The Doll People
Set Sail

WILSON & SONS CATALOGUE

BABY DOLLS

ASSORTED SIZES

ll-jointed

PAPA DOLLS

26135. Dressed doll with bisque head and limbs. Finest checkered suit. Height: four inches. Price.....$1.25

26136. Same as above with top hat vercoat. $2.00

GIRL D

26139.

popu

Fine

ribbon

painted y

hair. Ful

sleeves an

undertrimmin

Price.....$1.00

26140. Same as above but with pink party outfit and yellow toy balloon. Price.....$1.25

r quality
head, wool
75

e dress
ow.
50

MAMA DOLLS

26137. Finest muslin and lace dress. Bisque head with painted hair. Smooth finish. Bisque hands nd legs. ice.....$1.50

BOY DOLLS

26141. Bisque head and limbs with fashion- able sailor suit. Price.....$0.95

Other mama dolls
ious styles in
nd hair.
50 each

TINY BOOKS

26142. r
bindings.
Many titl

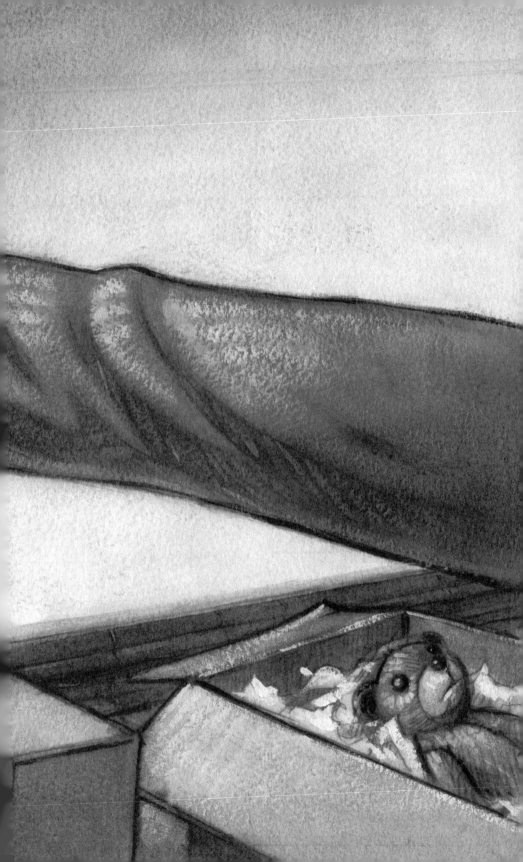

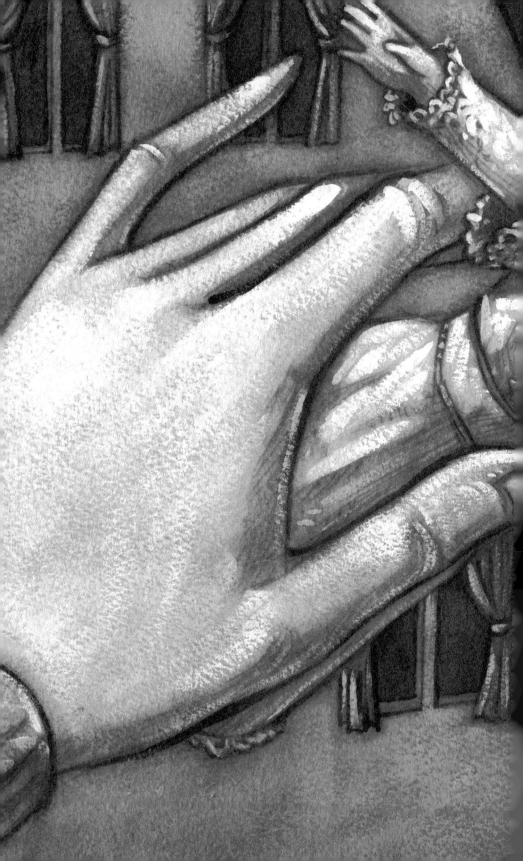

PEOPLE SAIL

ILLUSTRATED by BRETT HELQUIST

ATTIC

Disney · HYPERION

Los Angeles   New York

The series format, dollhouse, and character design of the original Funcraft and Doll families were established by Brian Selznick, who illustrated the first three books in the Doll People series.

Text copyright © 2014 by Ann M. Martin and Laura Godwin
Illustrations copyright © 2014 by Brett Helquist

First Edition
1 3 5 7 9 10 8 6 4 2
G475-5664-5-14196
Printed in the United States of America

Library of Congress Cataloging-in-Publication Data
Martin, Ann M., 1955- author.
The Doll people set sail / by Ann M. Martin and Laura Godwin ; with pictures by Brett Helquist. — First edition.
pages cm. — (The Doll people ; 4)
Summary: "Annabelle Doll, Tiffany Funcraft, and their families journey far from home"— Provided by publisher.
ISBN 978-1-4231-3683-5 — ISBN 1-4231-3683-7
[1. Dolls—Fiction. 2. Sea stories.] I. Godwin, Laura, author.
II. Helquist, Brett, illustrator. III. Title.
PZ7.M3567585Dr 2014
[Fic]—dc23   2013041937
Reinforced binding
Visit www.DisneyBooks.com

SUSTAINABLE FORESTRY INITIATIVE   Certified Sourcing
www.sfiprogram.org
SFI-00993

THIS LABEL APPLIES TO TEXT STOCK

Contents

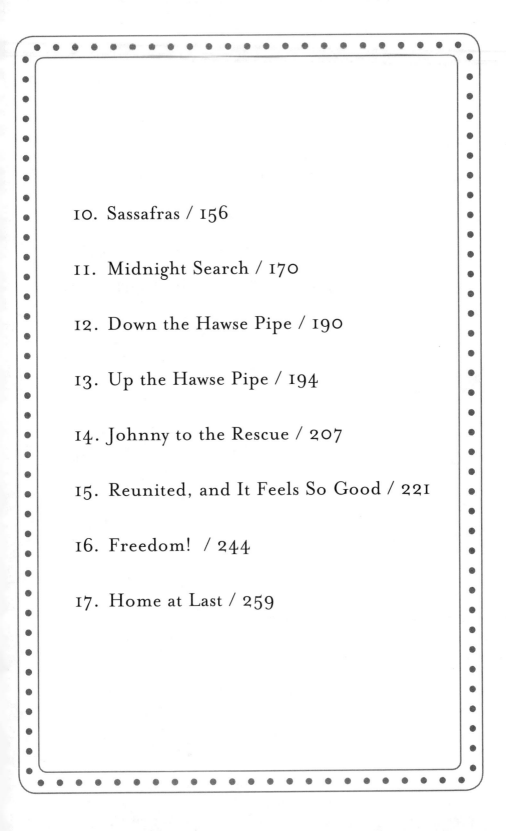

The Doll People
Set Sail

Punished

I F ANNABELLE DOLL had known that the biggest adventure of her life—an adventure both terrifying and exhilarating—lay only a week away, she wouldn't have believed it. This was because she'd just *been* on an unexpected adventure, and also because it was hard to concentrate on any thought when she was being flown through the air like a bumblebee by a sticky six-year-old.

"Bzzzzzzz! Bzzzzzzz!" Nora Palmer said

I

loudly as she whooshed Annabelle in dizzying arcs through the hallway, into her sister Kate's room, past a window, and back into the hallway. Annabelle could smell marshmallow on Nora's fingers. "Bzzzzz, bzzzzz, little bee. What are you doing inside on a nice summer day? You're supposed to be outside with the flowers. Be careful or someone will swat you." Nora paused. "I got a Fairy Swatter for my birthday, you know. It would work just fine with bees."

Except that I'm a doll, not a bee, thought Annabelle as Nora buzzed her once again through Kate's room and past the Dolls' house, where she could see her porcelain family posed stiffly in the spots where Kate had left them earlier. Annabelle tried to catch her brother's eye, but Bobby knew better than to move when a human was present. He refused to turn his head even a fraction of an inch.

Annabelle was then whisked back down the hall, into Nora's room, and over the Funcrafts' house, where Nora had tossed Annabelle's best doll friend, Tiffany Funcraft, onto the roof. Annabelle could tell that Tiffany was trying hard not to smile. She was sure Tiffany would love to be flying around the Palmers' second floor like an overgrown bee. That was just the kind of doll Tiffany was—adventurous and brave, traits Annabelle was slightly envious of. But Tiffany could afford to be adventurous and brave. Unlike Annabelle, she was made entirely of plastic, so she was both unbreakable and washable. Tiffany thought she was invincible.

Annabelle Doll, on the other hand, was not only made of porcelain—fragile, breakable porcelain—but she was over one hundred years old. Her fussy clothes were beribboned and lacy, and some of the stitching was starting to pull loose. If anyone should be flying through the air, it was one of the Funcrafts, not Annabelle. But Nora Palmer didn't think of things like that.

Kate Palmer did, though.

"Nora!" Kate's voice exclaimed suddenly. "What on earth are you doing with Annabelle? Put her down right now."

Nora let Annabelle dangle from her fingers as if she were going to drop her, and Kate shrieked. (Annabelle shrieked silently, imagining herself hitting the wooden floor and smashing into tiny china bits.) Then Kate whisked Annabelle away from her little sister and carried her gently back to the Dolls' house, where she settled her on a bed in the nursery.

"There you go, Annabelle," she said. "Sorry about that." She regarded Annabelle and her family: Mama and Papa Doll, who were sitting primly on the couch in the parlor; Uncle Doll and Auntie Sarah, who were midway up the staircase to the second floor; Bobby, who was propped against the bookcase in the library; and Nanny, who was watching over Tilly May and Baby Betsy in the kitchen.

"Dolls," Kate continued, "I need to have a talk with you. I have something important to say. There's going to be a big change—"

"Kate!" called Mrs. Palmer from downstairs. "Could you and Nora come here for a minute, please?"

"Okay!" Kate called back. She glanced into the dollhouse again. "I'll tell you later," she said hastily, and hurried from the room.

Uh-oh, Annabelle thought nervously. A big change. That doesn't sound good. As soon as she had heard two pairs of feet run down the stairs, she leaned over the edge of the dollhouse and called, "Mama? What—"

"Annabelle!" her mother replied in a shocked whisper. "For heaven's sake! No talking now. What are you thinking?"

"Yeah, we're already being punished," said Bobby from the library. "And it's all your fault."

Annabelle fell silent.

She'd forgotten about the punishment while she was being zoomed through the air. Now she lay miserably on her bed and kicked at a rocking horse. She was embarrassed about the punishment, mad at her parents, and also mad at herself.

"Annabelle," her mother said softly from below. "I can hear you kicking. Please stop that. If you damage the rocking horse, you're going to be in even more trouble."

Although Annabelle had been a living doll for over a hundred years, she had rarely been in trouble. She was cautious and tried to follow rules and obey her parents. But she couldn't be good all the time.

At least she wasn't the only doll who was in trouble. Bobby was being punished too, and so were Tiffany and Bailey Funcraft. They had all gotten in trouble together, and their punishment was that Annabelle and Bobby couldn't see Tiffany and Bailey for an entire month. And there were still three weeks left in that month.

"You know, Annabelle—" said Bobby from his place in the library.

Annabelle knew exactly what her brother was going to say. "I didn't tell you and Bailey to follow us outside!" she exclaimed.

"No, but lucky for you we did anyway. Otherwise you and Tiffany would probably still be wandering around somewhere with Tilly. You would never have found your way home again. And anyway, you shouldn't have left the Palmers' house in the first place."

"Are you fighting?" Tilly May called from the kitchen.

"Yes, they are," Mama Doll answered, "and if they don't stop, there are going to be consequences."

"Ooh," said Tilly.

"And may I remind you," added Papa Doll, "that *none* of you is supposed to be speaking now? You're all risking Doll State,

6

and that includes you, Tilly. So not another word. And I mean it."

Annabelle flopped onto her bed again. She thought back to the day—had it really been only a few weeks earlier?—when she and Tiffany had celebrated because Kate Palmer and her family, the humans who owned the big house, had left for a two-week vacation. Annabelle loved Kate, but the thought of two whole weeks in which she and Tiffany could play in the Dolls' old Victorian home and the Funcrafts' pink plastic dream house and, more importantly, anywhere at all in the Palmers' giant human house, had been unimaginably wonderful. Upstairs, downstairs, in the attic. Fourteen days in which they could do whatever they pleased and not have to worry about being seen by humans or discovered by The Captain, the Palmers' cat, who was a menace to all dolls.

And what was the very first thing that had happened? Tiffany had shown Annabelle a strange package that had arrived in the mail. When they'd investigated it, they'd heard a tiny, confused voice from inside the box calling, "Hello?" And that little voice—Tilly's, as it turned out—had set an adventure in motion, as if someone had tapped a domino and the whole row had tumbled over, one block after the other.

Annabelle sighed (but not too loudly), and thought about what she and Tiffany and Bobby and Bailey and Tilly had done. They had actually, on purpose, *run away* and ventured Outdoors into the enormous world of the humans. This was exactly the kind of thing Tiffany loved to do, and exactly the kind of thing Annabelle almost never dared to do, but she had done it for the sake of her little sister.

And now something else was about to happen. Kate had said a change was coming. A big change. Annabelle didn't like big changes in the humans' lives, not if they might affect the dolls' lives. Worry bloomed in Annabelle's mind. Kate hadn't played with the Dolls or the dollhouse very often that summer. Was Kate getting too old for dolls? What happened to dolls when their owners outgrew them? Annabelle had assumed that she and her family would always live here in this room in the Palmers' house. After all, long before Kate had been born, the Dolls had belonged to Kate's great-grandmother, and then to Grandma Katherine, and after that to Mrs. Palmer, Kate's mother. But what if Kate didn't have a daughter of her own, and one day she gave the Dolls away? What if she decided she didn't want them anymore, and she gave them away this very summer?

A night of worrying and fretting passed. Then, early the next morning, Kate awoke, sat up in her bed across the room from Annabelle's house, and said, "Dollies? This is a big day."

Annabelle's mind snapped to attention.

Kate stretched and stood up. She walked to the shelf where the Dolls' house had sat since 1898, when Kate's great-grandmother had been a little girl and this had been *her* bedroom.

"Today I have to pack you up—all of you, your house too—and send you away for a while. I'm really sorry about that."

I am actually having a heart attack, thought Annabelle when she heard Kate's words. The Palmers were going to move. She just knew it. What would happen to the Dolls? What if Kate stuffed Annabelle and her family into a packing carton that sat in a garage or a storage room or a stifling attic . . . and then she forgot about them? That would be worse—far worse—than being given away.

"It's only for a little while," Kate was saying. "Just a few weeks. Mom and Dad decided to have all our bedrooms renovated—that means fixed up and given a makeover. We have to clear everything out of the bedrooms and put all the furniture in storage. You aren't going to the storage place, though. You're just going to the attic. But I still have to pack you up. Don't worry, I'll pack very carefully. Oh, and in case you're wondering, Nora and I are going to stay in the guest room until the renovation is finished, but first we're all going to visit Mom's cousin Hugh. He lives in Wyoming. On a ranch. A *dude* ranch. We'll get to ride horses and eat beans around a camp-fire under the stars." Kate paused. "All right. I'm going to go have breakfast. But then I'll be back. Mom wants Nora and me to start packing up our rooms today."

Kate found her slippers and scuffed away.

The moment she was gone, Annabelle let out a tiny shriek.

"Annabelle!" said her father with a gasp, and Annabelle heard a similar gasp from Nanny, who took care of Annabelle and her brother and sisters.

"But I don't want to get stuck in a box for weeks!" cried Annabelle, leaping to her feet.

"Annabelle, hush!" exclaimed her mother. "And please sit down."

"But, Mama, we have to talk about this. We're going to get packed up and left in the attic for *weeks*? That's horrible!"

"Honey, there's nothing we can do about it," Auntie Sarah called reasonably from the staircase.

And Tilly added, "I was in a box for a hundred years. More than a hundred years, I fink."

"What if Kate comes back from the trip feeling grown-up and decides to leave us in the attic?" said Annabelle.

A footstep sounded in the hall outside Kate's bedroom, and Annabelle froze automatically.

"We'll talk about it tonight, if you like," Mama whispered.

"From inside a box," Annabelle grumbled, but she settled herself quietly on her bed.

For the rest of that horrible day Annabelle could do nothing but watch the chaos that unfolded around her. It began after breakfast when Kate returned to her room, followed by her mother. "Remember," said Mrs. Palmer, "that I would like you and Nora to sort out some of your old toys and clothes while you're packing. Put the throwaway things in the garbage bags, the giveaway things in the boxes marked 'ATC,' and the things you want to keep in the boxes marked 'Attic.' Dad and I will seal the boxes up later."

"Okay," said Kate, and then added, "Mom, what *is* ATC?"

"Allied Transatlantic Charities," her mother replied. "For children all over the world who need food and clothes and who don't have any toys."

Kate set to work. Annabelle watched from the nursery of the dollhouse as she slid an empty carton across the floor and began to place things inside it: her old Candy Land game, a stuffed goose wearing a bonnet, a jump rope, a box of pickup sticks, a pile of puzzles. Annabelle smiled to herself. That must be an attic box, since those were some of Kate's favorite toys. Then Kate raised one flap and Annabelle saw the letters *ATC* in bold writing, and she nearly screamed again.

Later, Nora barged into the room and poked through the ATC box. "You're giving these things away, Kate?" she said. "What if I want them? I still like to play Candy Land . . . sometimes."

"No, you don't," said Kate. "You've outgrown it. We've both outgrown all these things. Anyway, remember what Mom and

Dad said. We have to think of the kids who don't have any toys. They need these way more than we do. We have to be generous."

"I know," said Nora.

It was after lunch when Kate stood in front of the Dolls' house and addressed Annabelle and her family again. "Well, it's time," she said gravely. "I'm really sorry I have to do this, but I don't have any choice."

She reached into the kitchen and gently picked up Nanny, Baby Betsy, and Tilly May. She set them in a little heap on the bedroom floor next to a carton. Then she plucked

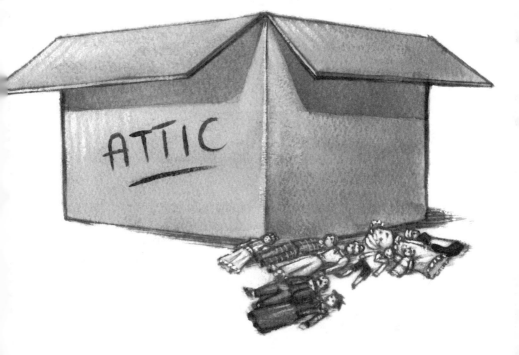

Mama, Papa, Auntie Sarah, Uncle Doll, Bobby, and finally Annabelle from other rooms in the dollhouse and placed them gently on the floor as well.

"Kate?" called Nora from the doorway. "Can I put my dollies in the box with yours?"

"Why?" asked Kate, sounding vaguely annoyed.

"Well, don't you think they'd all like to be together? They're going to be in the attic for a long time. They might get bored."

A little silence followed, and then Kate said, "Okay, fine. Leave them there by the box. I have to wrap my dolls in tissue paper. I'll put yours in on top of them when I'm done."

Annabelle wanted very much to laugh or to let out a shout of joy. Suddenly her weeks of confinement didn't seem so horrible. She and Tiffany were going to be packed up together in the very same box. Surely their parents couldn't forbid them to talk to each other.

Annabelle heard several small thumps as Nora dropped the Funcrafts—Tiffany, Bailey, Baby Britney, Mom, and Dad—onto the floor on the other side of the carton, and then the sound of Nora's footsteps as she left Kate's room.

"Bye, dollies," said Kate a few moments later, and the next thing Annabelle knew, she was being bundled into a sheet of tissue paper and turned over and over and over as Kate wound her up like a caterpillar in a cocoon. Then she was placed into the carton, and presently she felt gentle bumps as presumably the other members of her family were placed around her, although it was a little hard to tell what was going on from inside the layers of paper.

After that, nothing much seemed to happen for a very long time. Annabelle felt some more bumps and thought Kate had added the Funcrafts to the box. More time passed and she heard Kate say, "I'll just put these stuffed animals on top of you for added protection." Then the world became darker still, and quieter, and Annabelle realized that she didn't know what time it was or even whether it was day or night. She tried calling out in her tiniest voice, just to see what would happen. "Mama?"

But there was no answer, and Annabelle fell silent.

After another endless length of time (hours? days?) Annabelle heard Tiffany's voice from above her. "Everybody?" Tiffany said quietly. When there was no response, she said more loudly, *"Everybody?"*

"SHHH!"

(Annabelle thought that was Uncle Doll, although it was hard to tell.)

"But it's nighttime," said Tiffany.

"How do you know?" asked Mama, her voice muffled by paper.

Mom Funcraft's voice floated down through the layers of tissue. "There's a little rip in one seam of the box," she said. "We can see out."

"And it's the middle of the night," said Tiffany. "The Palmers are asleep."

So the adults held a discussion and this led to the first piece of good news Annabelle had heard since Kate had announced that a change was coming. "Your punishment is over," said Dad Funcraft.

"For all of us?" Bobby wanted to know.

"For all of you," agreed Papa Doll.

The next day, instead of being carted upstairs to the stifling attic full of spiders— spiders that Auntie Sarah admired and that Annabelle feared would creep into their box through the ripped seam—the dolls' carton was left on the floor. There was a flurry of excited activity as the Palmers packed up the bedrooms and got ready for their trip to the dude ranch. Annabelle breathed a sigh of relief.

But one morning—Annabelle wasn't sure which morning because time passed slowly in the dark carton—Mrs. Palmer came into Kate's room with a large roll of tape (according to Tiffany, who was spying through the ripped seam), and Annabelle knew it wouldn't be long before the attic confinement began. "This is it," she whispered.

From above her she heard Tiffany whisper back, "At least we didn't get put in a giveaway box."

CHAPTER TWO

A Serious Mistake

ANNABELLE HEARD A loud ripping sound—*RRRREEEEEEEECH*—and then the softer sound of a pair of scissors snipping something in two, and she waited to feel the jostling of the carton as Mrs. Palmer began to tape it up for its trip to the attic. Instead she heard another sound: Kate's voice. "Mom, wait! I forgot to put something in the box. It's the sweater I've been knitting for Annabelle. Please let me put it on her before you seal up the carton."

The next thing Annabelle knew, the carton had been reopened, and Kate's hands

2 I

were tossing out the stuffed animals and the Funcrafts, and some games and small toys as well, and then Annabelle was being unwound from her tissue paper in a great big hurry, tumbling over and over as if she were rolling down a hill.

"Here, Annabelle," said Kate as the paper fell away, and Annabelle tried to adjust her eyes to the light. "I made you something special. Grandma Katherine is helping me with my knitting, and this is my first sweater. I'll put it on you so you'll be nice and cozy while you're packed away. Let me just stick your arm in here. Huh. That's not the sleeve, that's a hole. Oh, well. And I'm sorry, but the collar is sort of coming off. And these holes over here are buttonholes, supposedly. I had such a hard time find ing buttons small enough for them. Hmm, what's this string hanging down from the bottom? I'll bet I was supposed to weave it in somewhere so it didn't show. Well, I'll have to fix everything after our trip. But I hope you enjoy your new sweater. Okay. Back in the paper you go."

Moments later, Annabelle was nestled in her tissue paper cocoon again, and she and the Funcrafts, and the games and toys and stuffed animals, had been returned to the carton. Annabelle stared into nothingness, feeling uncomfortably warm and itchy in the sweater. She wanted to complain to someone, but Mrs. Palmer was nearby, busily sealing up cartons, so Annabelle had to keep her thoughts to herself.

She recalled the first time she'd been trapped in a box—more than a hundred years earlier, when she and her family had traveled on a ship from England to the United States after they'd left the doll maker's shop in London. They'd been brand-new then— they'd hardly even known one another—and they hadn't realized that the youngest member of the family, Tilly May, had accidentally been switched with a baby from a much bigger set of dolls. The doll maker hadn't noticed his mistake either, and thought that the dolls he had packaged up were a complete and proper set. So he'd sent them off on their long trip across the Atlantic Ocean to the home of Mr. William Seaborn Cox of Connecticut, America.

Before their trip had begun, though, the Dolls had taken a secret oath. One by one, in the darkness of the workshop, a living doll had spoken to the newly completed dolls, explaining the importance of keeping their lives a secret. "If a human sees you moving or hears you speak," this doll had said, "or if you do anything to put the race of dolls in jeopardy, then you risk Doll State—or worse." Annabelle had still been in the sleepy, not-quite-conscious, new-doll trance in which she'd found herself when the doll maker had put the finishing touches on her that afternoon. But when it was her turn to take the oath, she had awakened sufficiently to repeat the Doll Code of Honor solemnly, saying dutifully, "I, Annabelle, an avowed member of the race of dolls, do hereby promise to protect our secret life by upholding the Doll Code of Honor in accordance with its ever-lasting law."

Doll State, which Annabelle had had

the misfortune of experiencing a number of times, rendered a living doll lifeless for twenty-four hours. What was worse was PDS. Permanent Doll State. Doll State forever. A doll plunged into PDS became an ordinary doll, no different from a doll who had never taken the oath, and slipped from semiconsciousness into lifelessness.

Annabelle didn't need to concern herself with PDS just now, though. Once her carton had been moved to the attic, no human would be able to see or hear her, so at the very least she and Tiffany could have endless conversations. They could make up stories and whisper secrets to each other and maybe coax brave Auntie Sarah into telling them about the many adventures she'd had exploring the Palmers' house. Including, Annabelle thought now, about the time she'd been trapped in the attic for forty-five years. If Auntie Sarah could survive that, and if Tilly May could endure her century of captivity, then surely Annabelle could survive being packed in a box for a few weeks.

The rest of the day passed slowly. Annabelle relied on Tiffany to tell her when night had fallen. And to catch her up on the events of the day, since Tiffany had spent the afternoon spying.

"Everything's all organized," Tiffany reported after she'd assured the dolls that the Palmers were asleep. "Mr. Palmer already took the garbage bags with the throwaway stuff downstairs. Tomorrow we'll be moved to the attic, and the ATC boxes will be put out on the front porch. They're supposed to get picked up in the morning. And at lunchtime the Palmers will leave for the airport."

"What about our houses?" Annabelle asked suddenly.

"Attic," replied Tiffany. "A lot of stuff is going to the attic."

Annabelle tried to relax in her cocoon, but she was hot and her sweater smelled funny and she felt jumpy and nervous.

The night passed as slowly as the day had.

The next morning started with a thump as Annabelle felt her carton being hefted into the air, and not in a gentle manner.

"We're late!" she heard Mrs. Palmer say.

"We overslept! How could we have overslept today of all days?"

"What time are the ATC people coming?" asked Mr. Palmer.

"They weren't sure. Sometime before noon. Hurry and help me move the boxes out of the girls' rooms. Leave the attic boxes in the hallway. We have to get the others downstairs and put the ATC labels on them."

There was a thump as the dolls' carton was set on the floor again, a lot of talking and rushing around and feet running up and down the stairs, and then Annabelle thought she heard the doorbell chime.

After that she distinctly heard Grandma Katherine call, "It's the ATC! They're already here. Are all the boxes downstairs?"

"One more to go!" Mr. Palmer replied.

A few moments later the dolls' box was lifted again, and Annabelle wondered why the Palmers were bothering to move the attic boxes upstairs when the ATC people were waiting downstairs. Her box was bounced along—there was the sound of feet on stairs again—and then Annabelle heard more voices. A man she didn't recognize said,

"Thank you," and then another man said, "Is that everything?" and Mr. Palmer replied, "I think so."

After a moment a door closed, and to Annabelle's surprise she heard Tiffany's voice from above her.

"We're outside!" Tiffany squeaked.

"No talking!" Uncle Doll said in a harsh whisper.

"But we're *outside!*" Tiffany repeated. "*Outdoors.* I'm positive. We're not in the attic. I can see grass."

"They must have mixed up the boxes!" said Mom Funcraft with a gasp.

"The Palmers were rushing," said Auntie Sarah, and Annabelle realized that this was such a big emergency that even the grown-ups were risking Doll State. "I'm sure our box is labeled 'Attic,'" Auntie Sarah continued. "Not 'ATC.'" Then she gasped. "Maybe in all their hurry, one of the Palmers mistook the word 'Attic' for the letters *ATC!*"

"The ATC people will notice that," said Bobby sensibly. "I'll bet they'll notice in just a minute. The Palmers didn't have time to put a label on our box. They couldn't have."

But no one noticed. Annabelle felt their box rise into the air again, and then it was shoved forward with a scraping sound and she was thrust backward into Tilly May's bundle of tissue paper, until at last the box came to a stop with a fast bump.

After that she heard the unmistakable clanking sound of a metal door closing.

An engine started.

"We're in a truck," said Tiffany, not even bothering to whisper. "We're being driven away."

"I fink we're in trouble," announced Tilly May as the truck bounced and jolted along a road.

"What do you see, Tiffany?" called Annabelle. The truck was so noisy that she had to yell to be heard, and even then she knew the deliverymen couldn't hear her.

"Nothing. It's completely dark. I think we're in the back of a van."

"Oh no, oh no," said Uncle Doll with a moan.

"How could this happen?" asked Papa Doll.

"To err is human," said Dad Funcraft.

"But what are we going to *do*?" Mama wanted to know.

"Nothing," replied Auntie Sarah. "There's not a thing we can do except wait and see what happens."

"Anyway, we've been in trouble before," said Tiffany. "Well, most of us have. And things always work out. What are we worrying about?"

Annabelle wanted to say, "What are we *worrying* about?" But since she was a worrier, and had been accused of worrying many, many times in her long life, she kept her mouth closed. Besides, Tiffany's attitude was much more refreshing. Tiffany, Annabelle decided, was the perfect best friend for a worrywart.

The dolls rode in silence for several minutes, and then Bailey called, "I think we're stopping! The truck is slowing down."

Sure enough, the truck came to a stop. Annabelle heard another clank as, she presumed, the van door was raised.

"Four boxes at this stop," she heard one of the men say. "They should be in the garage."

After a pause Annabelle heard some shuffling, and her box was jostled slightly as the four cartons were loaded onto the van.

"Two more stops," a man's voice said, "and then we'll go on to the warehouse."

"We're behind schedule. We were due back at the ATC an hour ago."

Annabelle couldn't hear the reply. The door clanged shut again and the motor roared. "The ATC!" she wailed, her worries flooding back in an instant. "We really are going to the ATC! We could wind up anywhere. Mrs. Palmer said the ATC donations are sent to children all around the world."

"But it sounds like we're going to a ware-house first," said Tiffany. "When they unload our box there, they'll see that we don't have an ATC label. I'm sure they'll return us then."

"Of course," said Nanny. "Of course." But Annabelle heard a quiver in her voice.

Annabelle tried to wait patiently while the van rattled along and more boxes were picked up. And she felt hopeful when at last she heard one of the men say, "That was it. Last pickup. Next stop is the warehouse and then we can go home."

"Okay," said Annabelle. "At the next stop

they'll discover the mistake. Right, Tiffany?"

"Yup." Tiffany sounded almost cheerful.

The van rumbled on. And on and on and on.

"How far are we going?" cried Bobby. "It seems like we've been traveling for hours."

"Do you think we're even in Connecticut anymore?" asked Mom Funcraft.

No one had an answer.

"Are you sure you can't see *anything* through the hole?" Annabelle called to Tiffany, and at that moment the van began to slow down again.

"Finally," said Bailey.

When the van had come to a stop, the door clanked open.

"Now I can see daylight," whispered Tiffany.

Annabelle heard scraping sounds and thumps, and soon the box containing the dolls was hoisted up and then set down roughly. She heard more clanking and foot-steps and lots of voices. The voices called out orders that made no sense to Annabelle. She heard the words "pallet" and "consolidation" and then someone shouted, "Hurry *up*!" in a manner that Annabelle felt was quite crabby and rude.

"Hey, look at this!" someone called suddenly, and Annabelle's heart leapt. The next words she expected to hear were *This box wasn't supposed to be delivered here.* Instead the voice said, "There's a rip in this carton. Better tape it up before it goes on the pallet."

"Darn!" exclaimed Tiffany a moment later. "My window is gone."

After that, so many things happened so quickly that Annabelle had a hard time imagining what was going on.

She heard someone shout, "Come on. Let's go, let's go!" She heard gears grinding and a motor revving, and she felt a bump and a lurch as her box was lifted into the air and then dropped with a thud. Then there was more thudding and bumping and jostling, and at last she felt movement again, and finally Bobby said, "I think we're in a bigger truck."

"But where are we going *now*?" cried Annabelle.

"It's a mystery," replied Tilly May.

"It's exciting!" said Tiffany.

* * *

Time passed. The truck rolled on. The dolls traveled in silence.

When at last the truck turned a corner, it continued on its way more slowly, and for the first time Annabelle could hear something other than the motor. From somewhere not far away came a mournful call.

"What was that?" asked Annabelle.

"I fink," said Tilly May, who, while trapped in her box for so long, had listened to a tape of birdcalls from around the world, "that that was the cry of a seagull."

"A seagull? Isn't that a shorebird?" asked Dad Funcraft.

"It is indeed."

"That doesn't seem right," said Papa.

The truck ground along on its slow journey. Now Annabelle could hear banging

and clanging of all kinds—quiet, deafening, distant, close at hand. And one unfamiliar sound after another.

"What's that whooshing?" asked Tiffany.

"Is it waves washing to shore?" replied Mama. "I seem to remember that sound from our voyage to America."

"And what's *that*?" asked Tilly May. "It goes OOH-ooh."

"It sounds a little like Nora," said Dad Funcraft thoughtfully, "when she's, well . . . gassy."

"Heavens!" exclaimed Mama Doll. "I don't believe we need to discuss gassiness."

"F-A-R-T-S," whispered Tiffany, and despite herself Annabelle let out a giggle.

"It's a foghorn," said Bobby. "A foghorn is making that sound."

Annabelle stopped laughing. Seagulls,

waves, foghorns. "What are we doing at the beach?" she asked.

No one answered.

The truck came to a stop. A few minutes later Annabelle once again heard a door clang open and felt the carton rise and fall.

"Hey!" exclaimed Tiffany. "Guess what. I just poked my hand through the tape. Now I can see out of the rip again. Maybe I can make the hole bigger."

Annabelle heard a subtle tearing sound. "Don't make it too much bigger, Tiffany," she said.

"I won't. I'm being careful. What does it matter anyway if—oops. Now it's a lot bigger. Oh, well. Hey, I can see . . . boats and—"

"Boats?" repeated Uncle Doll. "Plural?"

"Actually, they're more like ships. I think we're at a port."

"Yo!" someone shouted then. "Let's get going! All these ATC pallets are bound for *The Brown Pelican*. Let's get them ready to load."

And for what seemed to Annabelle like the millionth time that day, she felt her carton swing into the air with a lurch.

CHAPTER THREE

Dollies Overboard

WHEN THE CARTON had been set down again, Annabelle waited a moment before she said, "Tiffany? What can you see now?"

"In the distance—but not really too far away—I can see the ships. There are a lot of them, and they're big. Not like cruise ships we've seen on TV, but still pretty big. Each one is at a dock, and there are workers everywhere. There are people getting on and off the boats, too. Most of them are sailors. And there are cranes lifting boxes onto the ships. And not one box at a time, but lots of them tied together in stacks."

"Those stacks are on platforms called pallets," spoke up Bobby. "That's how things are packed for shipping—on pallets."

Nobody asked Bobby how he knew this. The dolls were used to Bobby and his facts. He absorbed information. "He has the brain of a scientist," Auntie Sarah had said once, and Annabelle was glad he did. His facts had been very helpful when the dolls had run away.

"Our box is probably on an ATC pallet now," Bobby was saying. "Can you see if there are any other pallets around us, Tiffany?"

Annabelle heard scratching and scrambling. "You aren't making the hole even bigger, are you, Tiffany?" she asked.

"I have to. It's the only way we'll know what's going on."

"Tiffany, seriously, you'd better stop. You don't want to make the hole *too* big. It'll be dangerous."

"Okay, okay, I'll stop. I'm done anyway. Wow, now I can see really well. And yes, Bobby, there are some pallets nearby, but I can't tell if our box is on a pallet. It probably is, though, because we're not on the ground. We're up in the air."

"I wish I could look out the hole," said Bobby.

"So do I," said Auntie Sarah. "And you know what? I think we Dolls should get out of this tissue paper. We need to be able to move around."

"Out of the question," Papa Doll said instantly.

"I disagree. This is an emergency," replied Auntie Sarah sharply. "We are not going to lie here wrapped in tissue paper waiting for something to happen. I think we may need to rescue ourselves, and we can't do that if we're wound up like mummies."

Nanny said timidly, "She's right. What's happened to us isn't our fault. We're not meant to be here. We're meant to be back at the Palmers' house. Kate will be very upset if she comes home from her vacation and finds that we're missing. It's up to us to fix the mistake."

"And risk Doll State?" said Papa Doll. "Or PDS?"

Another voice spoke up. "I agree with Auntie Sarah and Nanny," said Mama.

Annabelle couldn't believe her ears.

"And if we're going to save ourselves," Mama continued, "then we have to work together. Mrs. Funcraft? Could you and Mr. Funcraft help unroll us from the paper?"

What followed was a lot of shuffling around and rustling of tissue and unwinding and a series of worried yelps from Uncle Doll.

"Keep the paper neat!" cried Papa. "We may need to be wrapped up in it again."

Tiffany was the one

who unwound Annabelle, and when at last the paper had fallen away, she stared at her friend. "Is that the sweater Kate made?" Tiffany asked.

Annabelle nodded.

"Huh. I hope she doesn't make one for me. All right, let's unwind Tilly May."

When Tilly emerged from her cocoon she blinked her eyes and said, "Fank you. I do not like being all packed up."

"Poor Tilly," said Annabelle. "You *have* spent a lot of time packed up in boxes, haven't you?"

Tilly May, the little doll who had accidentally been switched with Baby Betsy, had lain lost and forgotten in a box in the doll maker's shop for more than a century before she had been discovered and eventually sent to the Palmers' house. Annabelle and Tiffany had come across the package and realized that inside was Annabelle's lost little sister, but Mama and Papa Doll hadn't believed them, so Annabelle and Tiffany had run away—in order to save Tilly May. Bobby and Bailey had followed them, and that was why they had all been punished.

"Annabelle, come *on*," said Tiffany impatiently. "How can you daydream at a time like this? Quit staring into space and help us unwrap the rest of your family."

When all the members of the Doll family had been freed from their wrappings, Auntie Sarah said, "I'd like to see out of your hole, Tiffany," and she began to crawl her way upward, past Annabelle and Tilly May, and through the layer of stuffed animals to the top of the box. Then she made her way to the split in the corner. "Goodness, Tiffany, you made quite a hole here!" she exclaimed.

"I know," said Tiffany proudly. "I made it big, then I made it bigger, and then the seam split and it just keeps splitting. It goes partway down the box now."

Auntie Sarah peered through the gaping hole as the rest of the Doll family members tunneled their way to the top of the carton.

"Don't let anything fall out of there!" called Uncle Doll, just as Annabelle said, "What do you see?"

"I'll tell you in a minute. What am I standing on?" asked Auntie Sarah.

"My ear," Uncle Doll replied grumpily.

"Sorry. Okay. Well, Tiffany is right. We're at a very busy port. Several of the ships are cargo ships, I think, and they're being loaded with freight." Auntie Sarah was halfway out of the hole, peering downward, when suddenly she was yanked forcefully back inside by Dad Funcraft.

"Sarah!" he exclaimed. "Watch yourself!"

"Sorry," she said. "I was just trying to get a better look around. We *are* on a pallet," she reported, "and I believe we're sitting on a loading dock."

"Then we're about to be loaded onto a boat," said Mama Doll tremulously. "Where on earth are we headed?"

"Could be anywhere," Dad Funcraft replied cheerfully.

"Our last voyage was six weeks of seasickness," said Mama Doll. "We can't go through that again!"

"It doesn't take six weeks to cross the Atlantic Ocean these days," said Bobby. "The same trip can be made in far less time. And most ocean trips are smoother now. You won't get seasick."

"I won't get seasick because I am not going on any boat."

"Well, I think an ocean voyage would be fun!" exclaimed Mom Funcraft. "Our family has never been on a ship before. We've never been anywhere before, unless you count our truck ride from the factory in Cleveland to the toy store in Connecticut. This is much more exciting.

Let *me* look through the hole now."

Auntie Sarah stepped off Uncle Doll's head and Mom Funcraft took her turn at the hole. "Look at those cranes!" she exclaimed. "I never knew they were so tall. The stacked pallets the cranes are loading onto the boats swing back and forth, back and forth, before they're set down. Back and forth, back and forth, swinging through the air."

"Stop!" called Mama. "You're making me seasick and we aren't even moving."

"But a crane ride would be fun too. Almost like flying! I can't wait for our turn."

"Mrs. Funcraft?" called Papa Doll. "Pardon my saying so, but I must remind you that we're not here for a holiday. We have to figure out how to get home *before* we swing through the air like monkeys and land on a ship."

Tiffany joined her mother at the hole. "I don't think there's going to be time to figure anything out. I think we're about to be—"

The rest of Tiffany's words were lost when the pallet was jerked upward so violently that everything in the dolls' box tumbled around—dolls and games and toys and discarded tissue paper—and Tiffany and her mother fell backward into the arms of a stuffed kitten. Then with a yank the pallet began to rise. Annabelle felt lighter, as if the bottom of the box were dropping away beneath her. The pallet rose and rose and rose, and then it began to glide through the air. The contents of the box shifted to the right, and Annabelle found herself squished between Bobby and a wad of paper.

"What's happening?" cried Annabelle.

Tiffany pushed herself away from the kitten and crawled back to the hole. "We're flying!" she exclaimed.

"We're flying! We're really flying!" called Mom Funcraft. "We're swinging out over the ocean."

"Now we're gliding past a ship," added Bailey. "I can see the name on the side. T-H-E," he spelled slowly as the dolls glided by, "B-R-O-W-N . . . P-E-L-I-C-A-N. *The Brown Pelican*."

"This is so much fun!" cried Dad Funcraft. "We're flying like birds!"

"This isn't fun! Help me!" Nanny started to say. "I—" But the rest of her words were lost as, without warning, everything in the box began to slide in the reverse direction.

Bobby was now pinned between Annabelle and the stuffed kitten. Nanny hurtled into Uncle Doll, Uncle Doll sailed into the side of the carton, animals and dolls shifted and lurched, and there was an awful ripping sound as the rest of the seam finally split apart and Tiffany's opening suddenly extended from the top of the box halfway toward the bottom.

Annabelle was clawing her way backward when Tilly May began to slide toward the hole. Annabelle pictured the ocean below, waiting to swallow her little sister. "Tilly!" she screamed. "Stop! Grab on to something!"

"I can't! I fink I'm—"

Annabelle lunged forward just in time to see Nanny heave herself away from a teddy bear like a swimmer pushing off from the side of a pool, grab Tilly from behind, and thrust her into Mama Doll's arms.

"That was close," said Annabelle, before she realized that Nanny was still in motion. She watched in horrified amazement as Nanny sailed smoothly through the hole and into the sky, disappearing from sight. The last thing Annabelle saw was the toe of one of Nanny's feet. "Nanny!" she shrieked. She tried to make her way to Mama and Tilly, but the pallet was swinging in smaller arcs now, moving from side to side, faster and faster, and Annabelle lost her footing and started to slide downward through drifts of tissue paper.

"Everyone stay away from the hole!" yelled Dad Funcraft. "Try to move to the other side of the—"

"Heeeeeeelp!"

Annabelle craned her neck upward in alarm and saw that Bailey was now careening toward the split seam. Dad Funcraft tackled him, grabbing his feet and clinging to them, but Bailey continued forward and shot

through the hole, with his father behind him, holding on to his shoes.

"Tiffany, no!" Annabelle shouted then, as she saw her friend clamber toward the hole. "Don't go near that. You'll fall out too."

"I have to see where they went," Tiffany cried, but Auntie Sarah caught her and shoved her back to Mom Funcraft.

Annabelle's eyes widened as she realized that Uncle Doll was now nearing the hole, bouncing along on wads of paper and the heads of stuffed animals like an astronaut walking on the moon.

"What are you doing?" she called. "Uncle Doll, what are you doing?"

Uncle Doll didn't answer. He grabbed at the tissue paper as he jounced forward, wadding it up into tight balls, and then he began to stuff it into the split seam. "Now everybody stay back," he commanded when the top of the hole had been plugged. He flopped onto a fuzzy chipmunk and began to cry.

Presently the swaying slowed, and eventually the pallet was set down on a solid surface.

Annabelle fell on her bottom and sat stock-still.

"We've landed," said Mom Funcraft.

Annabelle looked around her. The once neat box was now a mess of jumbled dolls and animals and toys, flecks of mangled tissue paper, and loose doll clothing. Tiffany had lost a shoe (which she later found wedged in the kitten's open mouth), and Uncle

Doll's necktie had loosened and come off. The box itself was misshapen, having been squished down along the split seam.

Annabelle sat where she had landed, cupped a hand to one ear, and listened. She could hear the ocean and the seagulls and voices, and some clanking and clanging and banging, but these noises seemed distant compared to the din she'd heard on the loading dock.

"Is anyone hurt?" Papa asked at last.

After a little silence Annabelle heard a chorus of quiet no's.

Then Auntie Sarah said, "We all saw Nanny and Bailey and Mr. Funcraft fall through the hole. Let's make sure the rest of us are here." Annabelle was relieved to find out that the remaining eleven dolls were all accounted for and all unharmed. What had been the fate of the missing dolls, though? Bailey and Dad Funcraft could float if they fell in the ocean and bounce if they landed on a boat—but how would Annabelle and the others manage to find them? And what about Nanny? She was as fragile as the rest of the Doll family. She might be cracked and chipped, lying on the deck of a ship, where she would surely be stepped on and smashed if no one noticed her. Annabelle decided that Nanny must have landed instead on something soft and out of sight. She must have. Annabelle couldn't consider any other possibility.

Around her the other dolls began to move about quietly. Mama and Papa cradled Baby Betsy, while Auntie Sarah sat Tilly in her lap. Mom Funcraft was threading her way through the tissue paper to Baby Britney when Annabelle heard Uncle Doll say quietly, "You shouldn't have enlarged the hole. What you did goes against every principle of dollkind."

There was a long pause before Tiffany replied in a small voice, "I—I just wanted to see what was outside. I wanted to answer Bobby's question. I didn't think anything would go wrong."

"But this is exactly why there are rules about interfering with the world of the humans."

Annabelle thought that Uncle Doll had more to say, but his voice was suddenly drowned out by a loud motor, and then the pallet began to move again. This time the dolls could only guess at what was happening, since Uncle Doll refused to let anyone near the opening. "Don't even *think* of pulling the paper out of the hole," he said.

The dolls sat quietly, whispering occasionally.

"Maybe Nanny landed in another box somewhere," said Mama hopefully.

"Impossible. The boxes are sealed," replied Papa.

"Ours isn't," said Uncle Doll crossly. "At least it isn't anymore." He glanced at Tiffany.

"I'll bet Dad and Bailey didn't fall very far," said Mom Funcraft.

"Maybe they're on top of a stack of boxes like ours," Tiffany ventured.

"For heaven's sake, they could be anywhere," said Uncle Doll. "Anywhere at all on the ship, or in the ocean. They sailed out into the open air."

At that the dolls lapsed into silence again. After what seemed like a very long time, Annabelle made her way to Tiffany and pulled her into the arms of the kitten. Tiffany burst into tears. "I've never done anything that got someone in trouble before," she wailed. "I never even have to be careful. Not really. I didn't think making the hole would . . . would lead to *this*. I only wanted to see what was going on."

"It wasn't your fault," Annabelle said loyally. "The box was ripped when Mrs. Palmer packed us into it."

"Yes, but it got taped up and then I stuck my hand through the tape. I made the hole even bigger. You told me to stop, Annabelle, and I went ahead anyway. And now look what's happened. Uncle Doll said—"

"Oh, don't listen to Uncle Doll. He's just upset. You know he isn't good in emergencies."

Tiffany didn't reply. She buried her face against the kitten and sobbed.

Annabelle sat in the dark box and worried about the missing dolls. She worried as she watched her father ignore Uncle Doll's pleas and finally remove one bit of tissue paper— just enough so that the dolls would be able to see out of a very small hole. She worried as the pallet with its boxes was unfastened from the crane and shifted onto something (Bobby guessed it was a forklift) and then moved off the deck of *The Brown Pelican*. She worried as the dolls began a trip through the ship: They disappeared down a ramp, along a corridor, and past portholes and doors, while sailors shouted and machine engines groaned and whined. She worried as they came to a stop and the pallet was lifted and then dropped one final time.

"Quit worrying," Bobby whispered to her.

"I can't. I just can't."

Annabelle was finally distracted from her thoughts when she heard someone say, "That does it for these pallets," and then the forklift roared away.

"Where are we?" asked Annabelle.

"In the hold," Bobby replied confidently. "This is where we'll be stowed during the voyage."

"I don't suppose there's any way we can get off the ship now, is there?" said Mama Doll in a dull voice.

"I don't think so," replied Papa.

Annabelle agreed with him. When she peered through the hole she saw nothing but a sea of cartons—carton stacked upon carton creating one tower after another—in an impossibly large space. "And even if we could find our way out of here," she said, "we couldn't leave the others behind."

Annabelle made her way back to the kitten and settled down next to Tiffany. "I have an idea," she said, putting her arm around her friend's shoulder. "I think it's time for SELMP again. We'll get everyone involved."

Tiffany stopped crying. "SELMP? I guess that could help."

At that moment Annabelle heard the blast of a horn and felt the ship begin to move slowly away from the dock.

The Doll People had set sail.

CHAPTER FOUR

Mission Impossible: Lost at Sea

NNABELLE AND TIFFANY were very proud of SELMP. It was a society—the Society for Exploration and the Location of Missing Persons—that they had founded themselves. Whenever a doll went missing, and this happened more often than you might think, Annabelle and Tiffany held meetings of SELMP, and they were amazed by what they could accomplish. They had originally created SELMP in order to locate Auntie Sarah, who had been missing for forty-five long years before they found her. And that had been just the beginning of their good work.

"I think we should invite our families to the SELMP meeting," Annabelle said now. "Don't you?"

"If we held a meeting here in the box it would be a little hard to keep it a secret anyway," said Tiffany, still sniffling. "Besides, we have a bigger job than usual. Three of us are missing." She paused. "Thanks to me."

"Well, thanks to a few other things too, such as swinging cranes and people who don't read box labels correctly. The hole was only part of the problem."

"I was the one who made it bigger."

"And you will help the rest of us find your father and Bailey and Nanny," said Annabelle, sounding much more certain than she felt. "Now come on. We have work to do. Are you with me?"

Tiffany sighed. "I guess so."

"So it's agreed. We'll invite everyone," said Annabelle.

"The babies and Tilly, too," said Tiffany, "even though they won't understand what's going on."

"Tilly might," Annabelle replied. "You never know."

"Now the first thing we should—"

"Shhh!" said Annabelle suddenly. "Quiet, Tiffany."

Tiffany looked wounded. "I'm sorry. I didn't mean to interrupt."

"It isn't that! Just be quiet for a minute. I hear something."

"What?"

"Little voices. And not from inside our box. Listen." Annabelle made her way to the hole and put her ear to it. Tiffany followed her. "Hear that?" asked Annabelle.

"How awfully exciting!" someone was saying.

"Invigorating!" said someone else. "The last cruise I was on didn't start out with nearly as much promise. Of course, that was almost fifty years ago, and I'm sure sea travel has changed a lot."

"All for the better," said the first voice.

"I say, do you think we can get out now? Maybe have a look round? I'd like to do some exploring."

Annabelle turned to Tiffany and whispered, "Who could they be?"

"Not sailors, that's for sure. The voices are too small for humans."

"Do you suppose," Annabelle ventured, hardly daring to complete her thought, "that there are other living dolls nearby?"

Tiffany widened her eyes. "There might be. Look at all the boxes down here. Who knows what's in them."

"But how could anyone be excited about this trip? If they're dolls and they're on our pallet in the hold of a ship, then it probably means they're being taken to the ATC and given away. That's awful." Annabelle lowered her voice. "Maybe they don't understand that they're being given away. Maybe they don't know any better."

Annabelle and Tiffany listened at the hole for a while longer, but the voices had quieted and they heard nothing further.

"What do you see out there?" asked a voice from behind Annabelle, and she jumped.

"Bobby!" she exclaimed.

"Sorry. I didn't mean to scare you. But what do you see?"

"Exactly what we saw the last time we looked out," muttered Tiffany.

"But I want details," said Bobby. "We need to gather information if we're going to save ourselves. We need facts."

Annabelle and Tiffany stepped away from the hole, and Bobby peered through it. He leaned forward and looked from left to right.

"Don't let anyone see you!" hissed Annabelle.

"There aren't any humans around," Bobby reported. He leaned out of the hole again. "Okay. I think our box is at the top of the stack. There are about six or seven boxes

underneath ours. Way, way over there"—
Bobby pointed to the right—"is a ramp."

Annabelle joined her brother at the hole.
"I think that's the ramp our pallet came down.
It must lead to an upper deck." She turned
back to Tiffany. "We're going to have to find
a way out of our box and up that ramp," she
said, "if we want to find Nanny, Bailey, and
your father."

"Then let's start the meeting," said
Tiffany.

Since most of the dolls had never been
involved in SELMP, Annabelle had to do a
bit of explaining before the meeting could
truly get under way. She was used to letting
Tiffany take charge of things and wanted to
do so now, but Tiffany was sitting at the back
of the group of dolls. In fact, she was sitting
behind Papa Doll, so that she was barely vis-
ible. And every time she managed to glimpse
Uncle Doll, she burst into tears.

Annabelle was on her own. "Well," she
began, and immediately hesitated. She peered
around her father and tried to signal to
Tiffany, but Tiffany sat with her head bowed,

so at last Annabelle said, "Um, okay, let's get started. First of all, we need to be able to work together. And not argue." (She glanced at Uncle Doll.) "Second, I guess we need a name for our mission. I was thinking of 'Mission Lost at Sea.'" She looked at the others, who nodded solemnly. "Third, we need a plan of action, although it's a little hard to figure out where to begin since we don't know much about the ship."

"Of course, when you think about it,

this is just like any rescue situation," Bobby interrupted helpfully. He turned to his sister. "Could I say something?"

"Go ahead," replied Annabelle, who added, turning to Mrs. Funcraft, "Bobby knows a lot about rescue missions."

"When a person is lost," Bobby began, "whether it's on land or at sea, the first thing the rescuers have to figure out is where to look, and that might not be obvious right away. But they have to start somewhere, and the important thing is to not get overwhelmed—and to not give up. You just have to keep going."

Annabelle saw Mama glance fondly at Bobby.

"Also, we need to make sure," Bobby continued, "that we don't get lost while we're trying to find the others."

"Oh," said Annabelle. "Right. Maybe we should do something to our box so we can tell it apart from all the others down here. No matter what, we'll have to be able to retrace our steps and find it again."

Annabelle expected Uncle Doll to object to this. She looked at him, waiting to hear him say, *Oh, no, no. We mustn't call attention to ourselves.* But he remained silent.

"What should we do?" Annabelle went on. "Any suggestions?" She peered around at Tiffany, who shrugged.

"How about a flag?" suggested Mom Funcraft. "We could fly it through the hole. That way we'd always recognize our box from the floor. Which, by the way, is a long way down from here."

"And we'll have to memorize some land-marks," said Annabelle. "That will make retracing our steps easier."

"All right. We'll do that the first time we go exploring," Auntie Sarah replied.

"Next," said Annabelle, "we need to try to figure out where Nanny and Bailey and Mr. Funcraft are, like Bobby said."

"How are we going to do that?" asked Papa. "They could be anywhere."

Bobby shook his head slowly. "Not really. Think back to when they went out of the hole. The hole was much bigger then. We could all see through it. Did anybody notice any-thing in particular at the exact moment when Nanny fell out? That might help us narrow our search for her."

"Oh, I see what you mean," said Mom Funcraft.

"I thought I saw a flagpole or a mast or something," said Annabelle, frowning, trying to remember. "Oh! And just before she went out, I saw some windows on *The Brown Pelican*. At least, I think they were windows."

Bobby brightened. "She must have fallen out above the bridge deck, then. That's the place in the middle of a ship where the wheel-house is."

"What's the wheelhouse?" asked Uncle Doll, looking impressed in spite of himself.

"It's sort of like the cockpit of a plane. It's where the captain sits when he steers the ship. He looks at charts and he figures out where in the ocean the ship is located and where he needs to go. That's a really good clue, Annabelle. That's where we'll start when we look for Nanny. And Bailey and his dad probably aren't too far away from her."

"Right after Nanny fell out," said Tiffany, finally daring to speak up, "I saw a big piece of equipment. I think it was part of a crane."

"That's another good clue!" said Bobby

excitedly, and Annabelle exclaimed, "Thanks, Tiffany!"

"If we don't find anyone near the wheel-house," Bobby continued, "we'll look by the crane next. That should be easy to find. We'll start at the wheelhouse, move on to the crane, and spread out from there, if we have to."

"My," said Mom Funcraft, "you certainly do know a lot about rescue."

Mama and Papa beamed, and Annabelle almost bragged that Bobby had been an awfully big help when they had all run away, but she decided it was better not to mention that particular adventure.

The SELMP meeting continued. After much discussion, Annabelle said, "I think we should split into two search parties. And one person in each group will be in charge of paying attention to landmarks. We're going to have to become familiar with the ship."

Bobby got to his feet. "Even a small cargo ship," he said, "is longer than a football field and at least as wide as three houses—human houses—and as high as a water tower."

Mama's eyes grew huge and frightened. "But that's enormous!" she cried. "How will we ever find our way around? We thought the Palmers' house was big."

"We don't have a choice," said Papa gravely. "Not if we want to find the others."

Mama pulled a hankie out of her pocket. She held it to her eyes.

"The more we can find out about the ship," said Annabelle, "the better."

"I think," said Auntie Sarah, resting her hand on Mama's back, "that the size of the ship will actually be in our favor during the mission."

Mama sniffled. "What do you mean?"

"The ship is *so* large and we're *so* small that I doubt anyone will even notice us. And if someone does see one of us, he'll probably assume we fell out of a shipping carton. Look at how many cartons are on board."

"If we see a human," said Mom Funcraft, "we should simply freeze in place. I think we'll be safe that way."

"But what do you think a sailor would do," said Mama nervously, "with a doll that was found lying around somewhere? Toss it into a garbage bin? Or *overboard*? That would be disastrous!"

"We have to try to stay out of sight," said Annabelle firmly. "Of course we do. Auntie Sarah didn't mean that Mission Lost at Sea would be easy. But I think it's possible. We can find Nanny and Bailey and Dad Funcraft." Annabelle turned to Tiffany. "Doll power!" she cried, raising her fist.

Tiffany gazed at her balefully.

Annabelle held up her fist again, this time higher. At last Tiffany raised hers too. "Doll power," she said in a small voice.

* * *

By the time the SELMP meeting concluded, the dolls had divided themselves into two search teams and decided to hold separate planning meetings. Annabelle and Tiffany were to join Auntie Sarah and Mom Funcraft to form Team Starboard. "Starboard is the right side of a ship," Annabelle said, "so we'll search that side. 'Port' means 'left,' and Mama and Papa and Bobby will form Team Port to search the left side."

Uncle Doll had chosen to not go through the hole at all and instead to stay behind with Baby Britney, Baby Betsy, and Tilly. Everyone, Annabelle realized, had a role to play in the rescue mission, and Uncle Doll seemed quite happy with his job as babysitter. He made a little tissue paper nest at the top of the carton, as far from the hole as he could manage, and he furnished it with some small toys he'd found with the stuffed animals.

Annabelle, Tiffany, Auntie Sarah, and Mom Funcraft chose a spot for themselves not far from the hole, resting comfortably on the head of a stuffed polar bear. Bobby, Mama, and Papa settled themselves a little distance away.

"So," said Mom Funcraft, "what will Team Starboard do first? Is there a SELMP protocol?"

"It depends on the situation," Annabelle replied. "In this case, I think we should do some planning first. We probably shouldn't go outside in broad daylight—"

"I'll say you shouldn't!" Uncle Doll shouted from the nest.

"*Ahem,*" said Auntie Sarah. "Let us do our jobs, dear."

When Uncle Doll didn't answer, Annabelle continued. "Since we should stay in the box until after dark, we have plenty of time for planning. I guess what we'll have to figure out is how to find our way to the ramp Bobby saw, the one that leads out of the hold to the upper levels. Then we'll have to figure out how to search the bridge deck and maybe even inside the wheelhouse. I think we're going to need a team leader, and that person should be Auntie Sarah, since she's already an experienced explorer. We need someone who can be in charge in a moment of crisis."

"Very efficient," agreed Mom. "Sarah should be our leader."

Auntie Sarah bowed her head modestly. "Thank you."

Annabelle decided that this was probably not the time to point out that while Auntie Sarah was indeed an experienced explorer, she was also the only one of all the dolls who had gotten lost for forty-five years. Instead she said, "And I think Mrs. Funcraft should be our scout, if we need one. She's not breakable—"

"Neither am I," said Tiffany, pouting.

"And she can bend and twist and get into small spaces to avoid being seen by humans—"

"So can I," said Tiffany.

"And she's an adult, so she'll probably be able to make better decisions about taking risks," Annabelle finished up.

Tiffany hung her head. "Not to mention that she didn't send three members of our families flying out into thin air."

"But," Annabelle went on, ignoring Tiffany's comment, "I think you should be the junior scout."

"Really?" said Tiffany.

"Absolutely."

"What about you, Annabelle?" asked Mom Funcraft. "What's your role?"

Annabelle squirmed. She didn't feel particularly brave. "I don't know."

"I do," said Auntie Sarah. "Annabelle should keep track of landmarks and any clues we find, and maybe even try to map the ship as we explore it. Annabelle is good at things like that."

Annabelle didn't know whether to be disappointed or flattered. Was this a lame job or an important one? She decided it didn't matter, as long as everyone worked together and they found the missing dolls. "Okay," she said at last. "Let's get to work."

By the end of the day—and the only way the dolls could tell evening had arrived was by a slight dimming of the light on the ramp leading down from the upper deck—the members of Team Starboard and Team Port had made plans and were anxious to start their Explorations. Mission Lost at Sea was about to begin. But before that could happen, they needed to find a way off the pallet and onto the floor of the hold. Annabelle leaned out of the hole.

The floor was a long, long way down.

CHAPTER FIVE

Strangers On Board

MOM FUNCRAFT, THE lead scout for Team Starboard, bounced over wads of tissue paper and joined Annabelle at the hole. Carefully she stuck her legs through the opening, and then sat down as if she were perched in the crook of a tree branch, feet dangling over the edge. She held on to the sides of the box and peered downward, examining the other cartons on the pallet.

"Careful!" Uncle Doll yelled from the nest.

Annabelle and Tiffany looked from Mom to the floor of the hold and back to Mom.

"Well," said Mom after a long time, "getting down isn't going to be easy, but we can do it. The boxes on the pallet are held together with strips of hard plastic. We can use the strips almost like rope. If we face the boxes, we can lower ourselves to the floor, hold-ing on to the strips with our hands and pushing off from the boxes with our feet. I'll go first, and, Tiffany, you should come right behind me. But first we'll throw down some of the tissue paper so that if one of you breakable dolls falls, you'll land on something soft. We—"

"Excuse me!" a voice called. "Before you do that, could you let us out of here?"

Annabelle looked around the box, saw nothing unusual, and then stuck her head through the hole next to Mom Funcraft.

Tiffany nudged her from behind. "That's one of the voices we heard earlier."

"But who *is* it?" said Annabelle.

"Excuse me, could you *please* come help us out of here? I don't mean to be impertinent—"

"*Non, vraiment!* Truly, he does not mean that. We've been listening to your plight—"

"And what a plight it is. But if you could give us a friendly hand, then *we'd* be free to help *you.*"

"Where are you?" asked Auntie Sarah, joining Mom Funcraft and Annabelle at the hole.

"*Je crois que nous sommes*—sorry, that is to say, I think that we—my friend and I—are in the box just below you."

"Are you . . . are you doll people?" asked Annabelle.

"Yes, of course. We thought that was understood."

"Well, we can't *see* you," said Tiffany.

"And it's better not to make assump-
tions," added Auntie Sarah.

"Forgive me. I am Tarquinius," said the
deeper of the two voices. "I hail from Great
Britain. Well, originally. Giselle and I have
been living in the United States for the past
five decades. In various homes."

"I'm Giselle," said the other voice.
"*Et je suis française. Comprenez-vous?* Do you
understand? I am French. Isn't this a grand
adventure? What I mean is that it's a grand
adventure for Quinnie and me, and it would
be a grand adventure for you if not for the
horrible misfortune that has befallen your
family members. Just think, Quinnie," she
continued cheerfully, "another cruise after all
these years!"

"But," said Annabelle, "aren't you in one
of the ATC boxes?"

"Of course. We're on your pallet, aren't
we?" replied Tarquinius.

"Then doesn't that mean you've been
given away?"

"Annabelle!" said Mama Doll with a
gasp.

"That is all right," said Giselle. "The

young lady is welcome to ask questions. And of course she is correct."

"However, the thing is, we don't feel that we've been given away so much as that we've been given a chance for re-homing," Tarquinius boomed.

"Yes, a new adventure! We are our own doll people setting out on a journey together. Very exciting. Very exciting indeed. *Peut-être* we will wind up back in my homeland for a while."

"At any rate, it isn't so much where we're going but the spirit in which we get there that matters."

"Goodness," murmured Papa Doll, who felt brave enough to approach the hole. He glanced back at the other members of Team Port, who were talking quietly with Uncle Doll.

"Now, we'd very much like to help you," said Giselle. "But we can't move. *Alors*, we are stuck in our box. Not the shipping carton, but the decorative case that houses us."

"And our case is under a pile of Barbies," Tarquinius added. "A rather large pile. They're dead weight. None of them has taken the oath, as you know."

No, thought Annabelle. Barbies never take the oath.

"So if you wouldn't mind digging us out," said Giselle, "we'd be much obliged. *Mais oui*, once we're free, we can give you a hand with your mission."

Annabelle looked at her mother and Mom Funcraft. "Can we help them?"

Mom peered down at the box below. "Their carton is crushed too," she said. "One corner is also split."

"Then let's see if we can get into the carton," said Annabelle.

"No!" cried Papa sternly.

"But they could help us," said Annabelle. "Just think—two more people to search for Bailey and Nanny and Mr. Funcraft."

"How about if Tiffany and I go?" suggested Mom Funcraft.

"I'm going with you," said Annabelle stoutly. Then she added, "And no one can stop me. This is important."

Annabelle waited for an argument from her parents. When they said nothing, she followed Tiffany and Mrs. Funcraft through the hole.

"Stick close to us," said Mom. "It isn't far. Hold on to the plastic and work your way down to the rip in the box below."

Annabelle did so, not daring to look at the floor. The moment her hands found the split in the carton, she wiggled inside after the Funcrafts.

"Whoa," said Tiffany under her breath. "Look at all these dolls."

"Someone must have been a doll collector," added Mom.

Annabelle stared around her. She saw a Russian doll, a Chinese doll, and a Swedish doll, all wearing traditional costumes. She saw a stack of nesting dolls painted to look like soldiers. But mostly she saw Barbies. Barbies of every kind. A 1960s Barbie in a miniskirt, a 1970s Barbie wearing bell bottoms, a 1980s Barbie in a business suit, a 1990s flight-attendant Barbie. Barbies, Barbies everywhere.

"Are *any* of you other dolls alive?" asked Tiffany in a hushed voice.

"Not a one!" shouted Tarquinius.

Annabelle, Tiffany, and Mom Funcraft dug their way down through the Barbies and had almost reached the bottom of the carton when they came across a doll, taller than Annabelle but not quite as tall as a Barbie, wearing what looked like a homemade superhero outfit: wrinkled brown tights (possibly castoffs from a Barbie), an oversized polka-dotted cape, and a white T-shirt with a big brown dot in the center. Over the dot were the letters *JOTS*.

"J-O-T-S," read Annabelle. "I wonder what that means."

The doll grasped Annabelle's hand and

shook it vigorously. "Johnny-on-the-Spot, at your service," he said enthusiastically.

"You're alive!" cried Annabelle.

"Someone else in this box, he is alive?" Giselle's voice called.

"It would take more than a little pile of dolls to squash me!" exclaimed Johnny.

"Oh, that's not what I meant," said Annabelle. "I meant that you're a living doll. Tarquinius and Giselle said they were the only living dolls in here."

"Who are Tarquinius and Giselle? Those loud dolls I keep hearing?"

"*Excusez-moi!*" cried Giselle.

"Over here!" said another voice.

"That must be Tarquinius," said Mom Funcraft.

"I'm not Tarquinius. My name is Otto."

"This is getting awfully confusing," said Annabelle.

"Don't you dolls all know each other?" asked Tiffany.

"No!" boomed Tarquinius. "Never met before in our lives. We were all left over from a neighborhood yard sale. Now, if anyone else in here is alive would you please speak up?"

Nothing.

"*D'accord,*" said Giselle. "All right. So it's just Johnny-on-the-Spot, Otto, and Quinnie and me. *Ça va*—the five of you should be able to open our case. Quinnie and I were jammed in here rather forcefully."

"I'd like to help, but I'm a little stuck," said Otto. "Sorry, but I can't move."

"I'll help you!" said Johnny-on-the-Spot. He dove under the flight-attendant Barbie and reemerged with a small doll in tow. The doll was wearing green lederhosen, a pointed green cap, and a tidy red bow tie.

"*Danke!*" said Otto, gazing at Johnny.

"What are you, German?" asked Tiffany.

"*Ja,*" Otto replied.

"*Now* will you come free us?" asked Tarquinius, who was beginning to sound impatient.

"We're on our way," said Johnny-on-the-Spot. "Dig, everybody!"

Annabelle, Tiffany, Mom, Johnny, and little Otto clawed their way down through the last few Barbies and reached the bottom of the shipping carton. Ordinarily Annabelle might have enjoyed the adventure. Certainly she would have enjoyed finding new friends. But her mind wasn't on friends. All she could think now was that they'd have four more doll people to help in our mission, and she tunneled ahead grimly.

She was mentally assigning the new dolls to Team Port and Team Starboard when she heard Johnny call, "Wow, is this your house?"

Annabelle found herself looking at a miniature Swiss chalet, a wooden box shaped like an upside-down *V* that lay at the very bottom of the carton. It was intricately painted: tiny, many-paned windows on either side of a red door, white flowers trailing around the edges of the chalet, and even a yellow bird perched on the roof. But near the top of the house were two real windows with wooden shutters that could open and close. And framed in each window was the face of a doll. They were rather large faces, and each took up the entire window.

Annabelle let out a squeak at the sight of two pairs of big, staring eyes.

"Well, don't just stand there. Let us out of this thing!" commanded Tarquinius, the face on the left. "The sooner we're out, the sooner we can help you."

"*Is* this your house?" asked Johnny again. "This box is your house?"

"*Mais non!* We are far too large for it," replied Giselle. "We barely fit in here. Perhaps it was once a box that held candy."

"I think it's safe to say that we were *stuffed* in here," added Tarquinius. "For safekeeping on our travels."

"Besides, we are not Swiss, either one of us."

"The important question is, can you get us out?"

The dolls crowded around the chalet.

"Hmm," said Mom Funcraft after a few moments. "I don't know."

"You're locked up tight," said Annabelle, disappointed. Her vision of returning triumphantly to her parents with four more searchers was vanishing rapidly. Johnny and Otto might join the search, but not these two spirited dolls.

"Of course we're locked up! That was the point," bellowed Tarquinius.

"I mean, you're locked up *very* tight," said Annabelle.

"Your house is like a cookie tin," added Mom. "The front of your house is jammed onto the back. I don't think we can pry the halves apart."

"Johnny could," said Otto. "He's a superhero."

Johnny looked pleased, and he examined the chalet. Finally he said, "I could do it, but I'd need my superhero tools, and I don't have them with me."

"*Ach,* too bad," said Otto.

From inside the chalet someone snorted.

"Could you crawl out the windows?" called Tiffany.

"Not a chance," said Tarquinius.

"You're certain?" asked Annabelle, but she already knew the answer.

"We could *peut-être* poke our heads out, but that is all," said Giselle. "We're far too big."

"Hmm," said Johnny. "Maybe if we work together we could at least push your house up to the top of the carton so you could look out through the hole. That way you could sort of be part of things, see what's going on. I think that's the best we can do."

"Better than nothing!" roared Tarquinius. "Let's get on with it, then."

This seemed pointless to Annabelle, but she didn't want to be rude to Giselle and Tarquinius, who might be able to help in SELMP's mission in some fashion, so she said nothing.

It took a lot of pushing and shoving and groaning and arguing—and almost half an hour—but eventually the five dolls managed to maneuver the chalet up through the pile of unblinking Barbie dolls and position it so that Giselle and Tarquinius were facing out of the hole and could see the hold of *The Brown Pelican*.

"*Désolée*, so sorry that we will not be able to search with you," remarked Giselle sadly.

"But Johnny and I can help," said Otto eagerly. "Especially Johnny."

And Annabelle suddenly felt a little thrill at the idea of a superhero joining one of the search parties.

She turned her attention back to the chalet and regarded the faces in the upper windows. Giselle's was sweet with kind brown eyes, high cheekbones, and rosy painted lips that smiled gently. Tarquinius, who was wearing spectacles, had ruddy cheeks, and eyebrows that would have been quite bushy if they had been made of real hair. His loud voice had unnerved Annabelle, but now he said to her softly, "Don't worry. I have every confidence that your friends will be found safe and sound."

"Thank you. And you will be able to help with the rescue," said Annabelle, turning to Giselle. "We need all the help we can get. We can use your brains, even if you are stuck in the chalet. And we can always use more friends."

CHAPTER SIX

Stranger Strangers

"HOW LONG UNTIL we can begin searching?" asked Annabelle a few minutes later.

"A few more hours at least," Auntie Sarah called from the box above.

"A few more *hours*?"

"Whining!" Auntie Sarah cautioned her. "You know very well that we can't leave until much later, when the ship is quieter and we'll be less likely to run into humans."

"Sorry." Annabelle flumped down

on a Barbie wearing a homemade green evening gown and put her chin in her hands.

"Well, don't waste time, girlie," Tarquinius boomed through his window. He turned his head upward. "Can you dolls up there hear me?"

"Um, yes," Mama Doll called down hesitantly.

"Righty-o. I think some introductions are in order. Everyone—introduce your-selves."

For quite a long time the dolls called to one another from box to box.

"This is Bobby! I'm Annabelle's brother."

"I am Giselle. I am Tarquinius's signifi-cant other."

And so on.

"Thank you," called Auntie Sarah at last. "And thank you for wanting to help us in our mission. We—"

She was interrupted by an eerie high-pitched howling that started out softly and grew steadily louder and more mournful.

"What on earth is that?" asked Mama Doll.

"I know this is strange," said Bobby,

"but it sounds like whales." He leaned out of Tiffany's hole and cupped his hand to his ear. "A pod of whales."

"Whales?" repeated Uncle Doll incredulously. "Oh, but it couldn't be."

"Why not?" Tarquinius's voice blasted out of the Swiss chalet. "We're on the ocean, aren't we?"

"But that sound is so close by," said Mom Funcraft.

The dolls stopped talking, and the howling eventually died away.

"Back to business!" said Tarquinius. "I think—"

He broke off as the mournful howling began again and seemed to swell up around the dolls.

"What *is* that?" exclaimed Annabelle, who was reminded of the moaning ghosts she'd heard in a scary movie that Kate had insisted on watching late one night with Annabelle sticking out of her bathrobe pocket.

"Could there be a whale on the ship?" asked Johnny. "Maybe it's down here in the hold with us, being transported to an aquarium or something."

The dolls paused to listen. The howling became louder than ever. Annabelle, still sitting next to the Swiss chalet, leaned out of the carton and peered downward. "You know," she said, pulling back, "I think the noise is coming from one of the other boxes on our pallet."

"Impossible!" roared Tarquinius. "There isn't room for a whale in one of these dinky cartons."

"There's no whale!" exclaimed Tiffany.

"*Mon Dieu,* we have a most interesting pallet, do we not?" remarked Giselle with satisfaction.

"Time for another excursion, Tiffany," said Mom, clapping her hands together. "Annabelle, will you come with us again?"

"Absolutely."

With much more confidence than before, Annabelle followed Tiffany and her mother down the plastic strips once more. They had gone no farther than the very next box when Mom exclaimed, "It's coming from in here. No wonder it was so loud. Whatever it is, it's right underneath Tarquinius and Giselle's box."

"And look," added Tiffany, "this box is split too."

"Nobody knows how to pack boxes properly these days," commented Mom Funcraft.

"That should make you feel better, Tiffany," said Annabelle.

"Sort of, I guess."

Mom and Annabelle and Tiffany crowded around the hole. The howling engulfed them.

"You know," said Annabelle after she had listened for a few moments, "I don't think this is howling. I think it's singing. I can almost make out words."

"Oh, look!" cried Tiffany, pointing. "*They're* the ones making the noise."

Annabelle peered inside the box and saw a clear plastic case. In it, lined up in a neat row like sardines in a tin, were . . . "Mermaids!"

"Goodness," said Mom Funcraft.

There were seven of them, four girl dolls and three boy dolls, all with red tails but with hair of varying bright colors, the girls' reaching all the way down to their ankles. The dolls had thrown their heads back and were chanting in unison.

When at last they stopped, Annabelle,

peeking through the hole, said politely, "Excuse me. We heard you, um, singing—we're from one of the cartons above you—and we thought we'd just come by and say hello."

"Hello," replied a violet-haired doll.

"Where did you say you're from?" asked another.

"The top carton," spoke up Tiffany. "Two cartons above you."

"Have you met any other merdolls?"

"Any other . . . whats?" said Annabelle.

"Merdolls. Mermaid dolls like us."

"Or mermen dolls like us," said one of the boys.

"Well, no. In fact, you're the first mer-dolls we've ever met in our whole lives."

The violet-haired doll sighed. "That's usually how it is," she said sadly. "There are so few of us."

"What are your names?" asked Mom Funcraft gently.

"I'm Freya. I'm the oldest. And this is my little sister, Seastar," said the violet-haired doll, putting her arm around the small-est mermaid. "That's Silver," she went on, pointing to a girl with glowing silvery hair, "and that's Pearl."

"I have a pearl necklace," Pearl announced proudly.

"Don't forget us," said one of the boys. "I'm Neptune, he's Poseidon, and the one on the end is Dylan."

"Hullo!" shouted Tarquinius. "What's going on down there?"

"I'll go let him know," Mom said to

Annabelle and Tiffany. "Will you girls be all right if I leave you here? Don't try to climb out of the box without telling me first."

"We won't," Tiffany promised, and Annabelle knew she meant it.

As soon as Mom Funcraft had left, Seastar sat up. "Are we allowed to get out of the case?" she asked her sister.

"I suppose so," replied Freya, and with that the merdolls slithered out of the plastic box. All except Freya, who looked nervously at Annabelle and Tiffany and said, "Are you sure it's all right to move around like this?"

"If we're careful," said Annabelle.

Freya began asking so many questions then that Annabelle felt breathless. "Where did you come from?" the merdoll wanted to know. "Were you given away? How did you get in our box?" And on and on. Finally Annabelle and Tiffany had to start at the beginning and tell her the entire story of their accidental trip in the ATC van, the transfer of their carton to the pallet, and of course the terrifying loss of Dad Funcraft, Bailey Funcraft, and Nanny.

"So we've formed search teams," Tiffany

finished up. "Team Port and Team Starboard. But we can't go out looking until later."

"We could help search too!" cried Freya. "We could form a posse of our own. An all-merdoll posse. If you're going to search the right and left sides of the ship, we could search the center."

"Um, well," sputtered Annabelle, and she couldn't help staring at Freya's tail and then looking behind her at the other mer-dolls, who were peering curiously through the hole into the hold of the ship, tails flapping behind them.

"Excuse me," said Tiffany, sounding uncomfortable, "but how, exactly, will you . . . I mean, that's a very nice offer."

Suddenly Freya began to laugh. "Oh, I understand," she said. "You think we can't get around. You are so sweet. Very kind and thoughtful. But, well, let me show you some-thing." She reached down and yanked at some snaps around her waist. To Annabelle's shock, Freya slipped off her sparkly red tail. "See? It's stretchy," she said brightly. "You just pull it on. We have legs underneath. Tails for water, legs for land, see?" Freya leaned around Annabelle and Tiffany. "Everybody, take off your tails," she called to the others, and in no time seven red tails had been tossed in the plastic box. (Annabelle was relieved to see that underneath the tails the merdolls were wearing bathing suits.)

"You mean, you can swim?" said Annabelle.

"Anyone can swim," scoffed Tiffany.

"But we can swim like mermaids. Living mermaids," said Freya. "We can live underwater."

Annabelle glanced at Tiffany and then back at Freya. "You believe in mermaids?" she asked.

"Of course. Don't you?"

"I guess so," said Annabelle.

"Um, I guess so," said Tiffany.

"Well, anyway, since mermaids can live underwater, I think merdolls can too," said Freya. "And now that we're on this ocean voyage we have an opportunity to make our home in the sea and start a merdoll colony."

"A merdoll colony? Under the sea?" Annabelle repeated, amazed. "You mean you don't want to live with a human? You don't want a home?"

"Of course we want a home," said Freya, sounding serious.

"But we want a proper merdoll home. And the only place for that is in the ocean."

"How exciting!" exclaimed Tiffany. "So you're going to jump overboard? When?"

"Well, that's the problem," Freya replied. She lowered her voice. "The others all look up to me. And I don't want them to know that I don't exactly have a plan. It would be so simple if we could just jump overboard, but we can't. For one thing, we'd get separated and we might not find each other again. Then there are the propellers. We could get sucked into them. Or we could be crushed by the boat. What we need is a way to lower ourselves down to the water and slide in gently without getting hurt. I'm not sure how we're going to do this, but it's been our lifelong dream and we have to make it happen. We just have to, and this is our only chance. When will we ever be on an ocean voyage again?"

"We'll help you," said Annabelle, glad to be distracted from the SELMP strategies. "Tell us about your plans."

Freya looked thoughtful, and then her face broke into a smile. "Well," she said excitedly, "what we would like is a merdoll ranch, an underwater merdoll kingdom where we can live forever." Suddenly she threw back her head and began to sing: "Seven seas, seven years, seven merdolls, seven tears. River to ocean: for water we yearn. Sorrow to joy, return, return!"

"That's our chant," she said. "It reminds us of the dream of our ranch. We'll ride sea horses—sidesaddle, of course, because of our tails—and gallop through the waves. We want to build the ranch in the shadow of a coral reef so the sea horses will have a corral. A coral corral. Our house will be made of sea-shells, and sea-glass pathways will lead from the bunkhouse to the corral. We'll use sea-weed for lassos and bridles. Our horses will roam free during the day, but at night we'll round them up and bring them home to the corral to protect them."

"Neptune and Dylan and I are going to form teams of sea horses that will pull us along in conch-shell chariots," said Poseidon.

"We hope to find other colonies of mer-men—" Neptune started to say.

"Probably they'll be real mermen, not merdolls," Dylan interrupted, "because they're aren't many of us merdolls around. We might be merdoll pioneers."

"—and we'll race against them," Neptune finished up.

"And," said Seastar, joining the conversation, "we're going to look for sunken treasure."

"What I most want to do," spoke up Pearl, sitting down between Freya and Annabelle, "is see a real mermaid. We've never seen one before, of course, and we're dying to. That's another one of our dreams."

"We're going to have a ranch house," Freya went on rapturously. "It's going to have curtains that will dance with the currents, and chandeliers that will glow with phosphorescence."

"And I'm going to find a sea unicorn," announced Seastar.

Freya shook her head at Annabelle and Tiffany and whispered, "She believes there are such things as sea unicorns."

"She sounds like my little sister Tilly May," Annabelle replied. "Tilly believes in unicorns too. Regular ones, I mean. We'll have to introduce Tilly May to Seastar."

"Did you know," said Pearl, "that if a mermaid who has been trapped on land cries seven teardrops, she can return to the ocean? But she can never go back to land again."

"We tried crying seven teardrops each," said Freya. "We hope that will help us find our way into the sea. And of course when we do, our tails should turn purple again."

"What?" said Annabelle.

"Our tails. They should turn purple again. We started off with tails that were purple and smelled of happiness. But because we haven't fulfilled our dream of living in the ocean, our tails have turned red and now they smell of sadness."

Tiffany leaned over and sniffed Freya's tail. "I don't smell anything," she said.

"You have to be a mermaid," Freya replied. "Anyway, I'm sure that if we can get safely into the sea, we'll have purple tails once more."

Annabelle gazed at her new friend. She was so engrossed in Freya's plans that she jumped when Mom Funcraft suddenly appeared in the hole, and she realized guiltily that her thoughts had been far from the plight of Nanny, Bailey, and Dad.

"It's time," Tiffany's mother announced. "We need to get organized."

A bell clanged then. "That's the midnight watch," called Bobby from above. "I think it's late enough so that we can search safely. Let's get going."

CHAPTER SEVEN

·

Out of the Box

THE DOLLS AND the Funcrafts returned to their carton, and the rescue teams—Team Starboard, Team Port (which now included both Johnny and Otto, since Otto refused to be separated from his own personal superhero), and Team Merdoll—each met briefly to finalize plans for the first search of the ship. Not twenty minutes had passed since the midnight watch bell had rung, when Bobby said, "We'd better move out. We don't want to waste any time. Is everybody ready?"

"Yes!" called the members of Team Starboard.

"Yes!" called the members of Team Port.

"Yes, yes, yes!" chanted the seven voices of Team Merdoll from below.

"I'll hold down the fort," said Uncle Doll glumly.

"That's a most important job," said Auntie Sarah. "Crucial."

"Giselle and I will give you a hand with it!" bellowed Tarquinius from inside the chalet. "Not sure what we can do except dispense advice, though."

"Good advice, he is always welcome," Giselle said stolidly.

Auntie Sarah regarded the other members of Team Starboard.

"Be brave," she said to them. "Be brave and smart. Think before you do anything. It's always better to be cautious, unless you're in immediate danger and have to act quickly.

"All right," she

continued, "Mrs. Funcraft, you go first, and
Tiffany, you follow her. But first let's throw
down some of the tissue paper. Enough to
soften the blow if anybody crash-lands, but
not enough to make the humans suspicious."

Once again, Mom and Tiffany made
their way down the plastic strips. Annabelle
thought Tiffany looked more at ease, having
practiced on the strips earlier. But it was still a

    very

    very

    very

    long

    way

    to

    the

    floor.

When at last the Funcrafts reached the
bottom, Tiffany leaned back and looked up at
their faraway carton. She grinned and flashed
the thumbs-up sign. Annabelle, Auntie
Sarah, and the members of Team Port waved
to her, and the rest of the dolls, followed by
Team Merdoll, made their way painstakingly
down the pallet and safely reached the floor
of the hold.

"Stuff the tissue paper between those two boxes," Papa whispered. "We might need it some other time."

Annabelle and Tiffany hid the paper, and the three search teams stood in nervous groups, surrounded by towers of boxes, like city tourists among skyscrapers.

"All right," said Bobby. "It's going to be a little hard to tell time on the ship unless we see clocks or computers or something, because the watch bell only rings every four hours. But let's try not to search longer than two hours tonight, since everything is new to us. Now, over there," he continued, pointing to one side of the ship, "is starboard. The other side is port, of course."

Annabelle looked up at the pallet. "Uncle Doll!" she called. "Are you ready with the flag?"

In answer, a tiny red-and-white flag appeared in the hole.

"Thank you!" said Annabelle. "Okay, teams, we'll meet back here in a couple of hours."

Team Starboard, with Mom Funcraft in the lead, began to edge toward the right side of the ship.

"Annabelle, remember to pay attention to everything we pass," said Auntie Sarah, "so that we can find our way back again. You're in charge of keeping track—"

"But it's even bigger down here than it looked from above!" cried Annabelle, starting to panic. "And it's dark and gloomy—"

"And you have a job," said Auntie Sarah.

"And we have to find my father and brother and Nanny," added Tiffany, "so let's get on with it."

Annabelle closed her mouth.

"Look!" exclaimed Mom Funcraft a few minutes later. "There are lights on the floor!"

Sure enough, Annabelle could see two rows of tiny lights illuminating the floor of the hold. "They sort of make a path," she said. "We should follow it. It must lead somewhere."

The four dolls began to walk between the strips of light, Annabelle looking at every pallet they passed, noting unusual words or pictures on the boxes, packing tape that was coming loose, stacks of boxes that were leaning, anything she could use as landmarks on the way back, when they were retracing their steps and heading toward their own carton.

"Up ahead is the ramp," Tiffany announced suddenly. "Bobby said it leads to the next level."

Annabelle looked over her shoulder one last time. Then the dolls, keeping close to the wall, began to ascend the ramp, leaving the hold behind.

It was like climbing a mountain.

"My land!" said Auntie Sarah, puffing. "This ramp didn't look so steep from the bottom."

Annabelle paused for a few moments, leaning against the wall and trying to catch her breath. "We're . . . only . . . halfway . . . there," she managed to say.

"Well, there's nothing to do but keep going," replied Mom, who was leaning over, hands on her knees. "Come on, everybody. And stick close to the wall. There's no place to hide here, so if we meet a human, get ready to flatten yourselves."

Once again the dolls set forth, this time walking in a tight line, one after the other.

"Left, right, left, right," said Tiffany.

Puff, puff, puff.

Annabelle stopped in her tracks. "What's that?" she whispered harshly.

The other dolls paused. In the distance was the sound of a motor.

"The ship's engine?" asked Mom.

"Not big enough," said Auntie Sarah. "I think maybe—"

Before she could finish her sentence they saw lights, and Annabelle realized

that a forklift was making its way down the
ramp.

"Flatten!" hissed
Mom, and the dolls flattened
themselves into the shadow of
the machine as it rumbled past.

"Do you think the driver saw us?" Tiffany whispered when the truck was out of sight.

"Not a chance," replied Mom. "The smallest wheels on the forklift were ten times taller than us."

"But that was a good lesson," said Auntie Sarah. "It was a reminder that we must be on our guard at all times."

Tiffany stepped away from the wall and peered up and down the ramp. "The coast is clear," she said softly.

"Onward!" was Auntie Sarah's quiet reply.

Hugging the wall, the dolls finally reached the top of the ramp.

"Now what?" asked Annabelle.

They had emerged into a dimly lit passage that stretched for a long way in either direction.

"Should we go right or left?" asked Mom.

"Don't we want to go up?" replied Annabelle. "I think we're still below the main deck. Nanny and the others must be above us on some level that's in the open air."

"I see another ramp," said Tiffany softly.

And so the exhausted dolls continued

walking and climbing until finally they reached . . .

"Open air!" said Annabelle with relief.

"Look!" Tiffany dared to cry. "There's a hole right here, and I can see the ocean through it!"

Sure enough, in the bulwarks surrounding the deck were a number of small holes just inches above the floor. When Annabelle joined Tiffany at the nearest one, she could see, in the bright light of a full moon, the broad expanse of the ocean. She drew in her breath.

"It's like magic," she whispered. "It's as big as the sky."

"I never," said Auntie Sarah from behind her. "The Atlantic Ocean. In all my born days . . ."

"Are those porpoises?" asked Mom Funcraft suddenly.

Annabelle saw a silvery splash as a sleek

body slipped below the surface of the water. "Porpoises," she breathed. "Imagine."

Annabelle could have gazed out at the sea and the moonlight and the wondrous water creatures forever, but Auntie Sarah said, "All right, Team Starboard. Time to continue our mission."

Reluctantly, Annabelle drew herself away from the hole and turned back to the ship. "Where do you think we are?" she asked.

"Exactly where Bobby wants us to be. That's the wheelhouse, isn't it?" said Mom Funcraft, pointing.

"And, look, there's a crane!" cried Annabelle. She couldn't see the platform of the crane, but the boom was suspended high above the other

end of the ship. It towered so far above her, in fact, that when she leaned back to look up at it, she fell over and landed on her bottom. Embarrassed, Annabelle glanced at Tiffany, expecting her to laugh, but Tiffany was staring at the deck, frowning. "What's this?" she asked, and she bent down to pick up a tiny object.

Annabelle took it and exclaimed, "That's Nanny's shoe!"

"Nanny doesn't wear shoes," said Tiffany. "Her shoes are painted on her feet."

Annabelle shook her head. "Kate bought a pair of old doll shoes at a yard sale. They're a bit big for Nanny, though, which is probably why this one fell off." She looked above her, expecting to see Nanny dangling from a pole or a rope, one shoe missing. But the only thing above her head was the starry sky.

The dolls tiptoed along the rough boards of the deck, Annabelle clutching Nanny's shoe. Tiffany and Mom and Auntie Sarah craned their necks upward (which caused Tiffany to trip frequently), but Annabelle kept her eyes to the floor, and so she was the one to cry suddenly, "There's Nanny's other shoe!"

Sure enough, the mate to the shoe Tiffany had found was lying next to a wooden crate. Annabelle looked farther along the deck. "And," she said breathlessly, running forward to retrieve something small and white, "this is . . ." She tried not to sob. "This is her cap."

The other dolls crowded around Annabelle's outstretched hands.

"Are you sure it's Nanny's?" asked Tiffany.

Auntie Sarah frowned. "It's Nanny's all right."

Annabelle glanced over her shoulder at the spot where Tiffany had found the first shoe. Her gaze traveled to the place where she had found the other shoe and from there to where they were now standing, examining the cap. She had just traced a neat line along the deck, from shoe to shoe to cap. She allowed her eyes to continue along the line and then to travel upward. Far above was the crane they had glimpsed earlier.

"Do you think—" Annabelle started to

say, but Tiffany clapped a hand over her mouth.

"*Shh!*" she said. "Does anyone else hear that?"

"I don't hear anything," said Mom.

"Listen very hard."

The dolls stood still and listened as hard as they could, and after a few moments Annabelle thought she heard a tiny voice call, "Here! I'm up here!"

"That's Nanny!" cried Annabelle. "It must be."

"But where is she?" said Mom.

Annabelle's eyes traveled once again to the crane. "I think I know." She pointed upward. An impossibly tiny figure was dangling precariously from the cable that was attached to the boom of the crane.

Tiffany gasped, and Mom whispered, "Oh no."

Auntie Sarah put her hand over her heart. "She's alive."

Annabelle ran full tilt across the deck until she was standing directly below Nanny. The other dolls followed her.

"We're going to get you down!" Annabelle

shouted, not caring how loud her voice sounded.

Nanny shouted something back, but her words were lost in a gust of wind that sent the cable swinging.

"What?" Annabelle yelled. "We can't hear you!" She paused, listening. "I'm sorry, Nanny," she said after a moment. "The wind is too strong." Then she added, "Climb down the cable! Come closer to us!"

Nanny waved one arm, but otherwise she didn't budge.

"Nanny, come on!" shouted Annabelle. "We're right here to help you. Climb down."

Nothing.

"I think she's stuck," said Tiffany after a moment. "The cable is braided. Maybe her dress is caught in it."

The dolls watched as Nanny reached down and began to tug at the hem of her dress. She tugged and tugged and—

"Hey, she's moving!" Mom Funcraft said. "I think she's climbing down after all."

Hope swelled in Annabelle's chest.

That was when she heard the voices. Deep human voices.

"Fix the winch *now*?" said one.

"Captain wants it done before morning," said another.

"What's a winch?" Annabelle whispered to Tiffany.

"Don't know."

The sailors disappeared from view. Annabelle turned to look at Nanny again, heard a grinding sound from the crane, and watched wide-eyed as the cable, with Nanny still clinging to it, suddenly began to rise.

"Noooo!" Annabelle moaned.

The cable continued to rise, and Nanny, no longer stuck, scrambled downward. But it was like trying to run up an escalator that was going in the opposite direction. And the cable was moving faster than Nanny was.

"What are we going to do?" wailed Annabelle.

"We need help," Auntie Sarah said grimly. "We can't rescue Nanny by ourselves. We have to find the others." She cupped her hands around her mouth, and even though Nanny wouldn't be able to hear her over the noise of the crane, she shouted, "Nanny, hang on tight! We're going to figure out how to rescue you. We'll be back as soon as we can."

"Let's go," said Mom. "Which direction did we come from?"

"Wait!" exclaimed Annabelle. "Before we leave, we should find some way to let the

others know that Nanny is here, just in case another team comes along later." She thought for a moment before removing the sash from her dress and tying it around the leg of a deck chair, at doll's-eye level. Then she grabbed up Nanny's shoes and cap and ran after the rest of Team Starboard.

CHAPTER EIGHT

Nanny: Missing in Action

THE DOLLS FOUND their way back to the hold of *The Brown Pelican*, moving as fast as they could, which wasn't very fast, even considering that the trip was mostly downhill. But at last they were once again among the towers of boxes.

"Annabelle, do you think you can find the route back to our pallet?" asked Mom Funcraft, studying the towers of boxes in the dim light.

Annabelle examined the nearest cartons and was relieved to recognize one with the words DOGS ARE PEOPLE TOO! printed across the side, and another on which someone had scrawled I LOVE LUCY CASSETTES.

"We're on the right track," she announced. "And look—there are the lights we followed."

The dolls hurried along the lighted path until Annabelle said, "I think we turn here."

After several more turns (four of them in the right direction, and one in the wrong direction), Annabelle said, "We're almost there."

Sure enough, the dolls were soon standing at the bottom of their pallet, looking up at Uncle Doll's flag.

"I wonder if anyone else is back yet," said Mom.

Tarquinius's voice suddenly bellowed down to them. "You're the first ones back!"

"Tarquinius! *S'il vous plaît.* Please keep your voice down," said Giselle more quietly. Then she called softly, "We haven't heard a thing from either of the other teams."

"Nothing?" wailed Annabelle. "But we need their help."

"Desperately," added Tiffany.

"You've been gone for hours," said Uncle Doll accusingly from the hole of the topmost carton.

"Never mind that," said Mom Funcraft. "We're late because we found Nanny. But she's in trouble and we need the others."

"You found Nanny?" cried Uncle Doll.

"Yes! She's caught on a crane way up high—"

"Shh! Shh!" said Auntie Sarah. "We can't shout the whole story right now. Someone might hear us. We'll have to tell you later."

Uncle Doll withdrew nervously inside the box.

The members of Team Starboard sat on

the floor of the hold and waited.

And waited.

And waited.

And waited.

"This is agony," moaned Tiffany. "I think we should go back to Nanny."

"And do what?" asked Mom Funcraft.

"Where could everyone else *be*?" said Annabelle.

"Maybe they got lost," said Mom.

"Maybe they're trapped somewhere," said Tiffany. "Or they had to hide from someone."

"Or," said Annabelle in an ominous tone, "maybe they're in Doll State."

"Let's hope not," said Mom.

Several more minutes passed, and finally Auntie Sarah said, "All right. I suppose we should go back to Nanny. I don't know what else to do. At least we know where she is. Maybe we'll run into some of the others on the way. If we don't go now, it will be light soon, and then we'll have to wait until tomorrow night to try again."

The four dolls set out once again on the journey to the upper deck. They managed to emerge at exactly the same spot as before, in sight of the wheelhouse. Now, though, they ran by the holes, ignoring the ocean and the sea creatures, and didn't stop until they were standing breathlessly below the crane. Annabelle closed her eyes briefly before she found the courage to tip her head back and look up. Please, please let Nanny be all right, she thought.

She looked at the cable swinging from the crane. She looked at the top where the cable met the boom, and her eyes followed the cable down to the bottom and back up again. "I don't see her," she whispered.

"Neither do I," said Mom Funcraft and Auntie Sarah at the same time.

The dolls looked at one another in horror.

Annabelle pictured Nanny losing her battle with the cable and finally being pulled up to the boom and threaded through the pulley. She hung her head.

"Maybe she fell," whispered Tiffany. "I think she fell." Tiffany sank onto the deck and began to cry. "She let go of the cable and she just fell. And it's all my fault."

Annabelle set her own horrible thoughts aside and put her arm around her friend. "You couldn't have known this would happen," she said. "It isn't as if you set out to hurt someone. And think about it, you found the first clue tonight. You found Nanny's shoe. If you hadn't seen that, we probably wouldn't have found her at all."

Mom Funcraft knelt next to Tiffany. "Let's think about this rationally," she said gently. "If she fell, where do you think she would have landed?"

Tiffany looked up at the crane and then down at the deck. "Right around here," she said at last.

The dolls scoured the deck, but they didn't see Nanny, and they didn't see anything that had belonged to her. "Well, it doesn't look as if she fell," Annabelle said at last. She glanced once more at the crane. I t was silent now, the cable motionless. Was it a good thing or a bad thing that she couldn't see a tiny doll anywhere at all on the cable or the boom?

"What should we do?" asked Mom.

The dolls shook their heads.

Nanny had disappeared.

And so had Annabelle's sash.

CHAPTER NINE

Rescued!

THE MEMBERS OF Team Starboard made their way anxiously down the levels and through the corridors of *The Brown Pelican* and then between the towers of boxes in the hold to their very own pallet. They looked up at the flag.

"Anyone back yet?" called Mom Funcraft.

"Not a one!" barked Tarquinius. "What happened to your two-hour time limit? It's practically daylight."

"*Mon cher,* I beg you, please keep your voice down!" said Giselle.

"Hee-hee, *we're* back!" called a small

voice. Annabelle turned around to see Team Merdoll approaching. "We've been following you," said Freya.

Annabelle ran to Freya and hugged her. "Oh, thank goodness," she said. "It's so late and no one else had come back and we found Nanny in a horrible mess but we had to leave her and now she's missing—"

"What? What?" said Freya.

Dylan exclaimed, "You found Nanny?"

And Silver cried, "What do you mean, you had to leave her and now she's missing?"

Annabelle took a deep breath and told the story of following Nanny's trail from her shoe to the crane, of watching help- lessly as Nanny was pulled upward toward the gears and pulleys on the boom, of leav- ing her there and going for help, and finally of returning to the crane to find Nanny gone. When she was finished she said, "And since neither of the other teams had returned, we thought something terrible had happened to all of you. But here you are. So maybe Team Port is okay too."

"But what could have happened to Nanny?" asked Neptune.

Annabelle shook her head. She didn't want to talk about the awful possibilities.

"We'd better go back up to our boxes," said Auntie Sarah. "The ship will be coming to life soon."

"But Bobby—" Annabelle started to say.

Auntie Sarah interrupted her with a shake of her head. "We can't worry about the others. We have to get out of sight. Now."

Team Starboard and Team Merdoll began the long climb up the cartons on the pallet.

"Come into our box for a

while, Freya," Annabelle said, puffing and out of breath, as they neared the top. "There's room for all of you. We can wait together there."

So the seven merdolls followed Team Starboard through the hole and into Annabelle's box.

"What's going on up there?" called Tarquinius presently.

"*Shhh!*" said Auntie Sarah. "You must learn to modulate your voice."

Annabelle answered Tarquinius quietly. "We're just waiting for the last team to come back."

Seastar had caught sight of Tilly May and begun crawling through the layers of tissue paper toward her when Tiffany exclaimed softly, "Hey!"

"What is it?" asked Annabelle.

Tiffany pulled her to the hole. "Listen."

Annabelle heard a scuffling that she thought might be tiny footsteps on the floor of the hold. She listened harder. And then she heard a voice call, "Ahoy!"

"Bobby?" said Annabelle. She leaned so far out of the hole that Auntie Sarah had to yank her back. "But it's Bobby! Team Port is here!"

"And we have Nanny," said Papa Doll proudly.

Annabelle, ignoring Auntie Sarah, leaned out of the hole again and stared downward. She could barely make out the members of Team Port.

From behind her came a huge commotion. Uncle Doll had followed Annabelle to the hole, and everyone was speaking at once.

"They found her?"

"Where was she?"

"Did she fall?"

"How on earth did you get her off the crane?"

"Is she all right?"

And then Tarquinius said, "You're making more noise up there than a bunch of crows! Wait until they've climbed back. Then they can tell their story."

Annabelle, shaking with excitement, grasped Tiffany's hand and watched the members of Team Port make their tired but triumphant way home. Otto came first, followed by Mama, then Papa, then Bobby, and

finally Johnny-on-the-Spot,
with his polka-dotted cape
now slung over one
shoulder.

"Where's Nanny?"
Annabelle called
anxiously.

"In here,"
Nanny replied
weakly from within
Johnny's bundle.

Everyone had more
questions, and Uncle Doll came close to falling through the hole himself as he leaned out
for a look at Nanny.

"Please! Everyone, calm down!" admon-
ished Auntie Sarah.

"That's an order!" added Tarquinius.

It was several more minutes before the
members of Team Port finally heaved themselves through the hole and into the carton.
Johnny set his bundle down gingerly on a pile
of tissue paper and untied it with great care.

There sat Nanny. Her dress was torn—
quite badly, too—and she was windblown
and smudged with dirt, and her shoes and

cap were missing, of course, but otherwise, thought Annabelle, she didn't look as if she had just spent hours dangling from a crane. (Although Annabelle wasn't sure what a doll person who had been dangling from a crane for hours *should* look like.)

"Oh, dear Nanny," said Auntie Sarah gently, and she sat down next to Nanny and put her arm across her shoulders.

An instant later the rest of the Doll family had crowded around them and were hugging Nanny and kissing her and telling her how brave she'd been. Annabelle handed Nanny her shoes and cap. Tiffany, Mom Funcraft, Johnny, Otto, and the merdolls stood back and watched solemnly. Annabelle listened for a bellowed question from Tarquinius, but for once no voices issued from the box below.

After the Dolls had assured themselves that Nanny was all in one piece (she wasn't even chipped, Annabelle noted with awe), the questions began again.

"How did you get off the cable, Nanny?"

"Did you fall off after we left? You couldn't have fallen."

Bobby held up his hands. "Wait! Wait!

Let Nanny rest for a minute. We know the story. We'll tell you what happened."

Nanny sat where she was, in the middle of Johnny's cape, saying nothing, her cheeks turning pink as she blinked back tears.

"All right," said Bobby to the crowd of dolls. "This is what happened: We'd been out searching forever and we hadn't seen Nanny or Bailey or Mr. Funcraft, so we were feeling discouraged and we decided to come back here. We'd gotten all turned around, though, and just when I realized that we were on the starboard side of the ship instead of the port side, I saw your sash, Annabelle." Bobby reached into his pocket for the sash and handed it back to his sister. "That was really smart," he told her. "We knew you'd been to that spot ahead of us and that it was important somehow. So we looked all around. We didn't see anything, but then we heard a voice calling to us."

"That was me," said Nanny weakly. "You'd already left," she added, turning to the members of Team Starboard.

"We'd found Nanny," Annabelle spoke up. "We'd followed her trail—her shoes and her cap—and we'd seen her dangling from the crane. Then the sailors started to pull the cable up to the boom, and we didn't know what to do. We just knew we needed more help if we were going to get her down. So we came back here, but everyone else was still out searching."

"You should all be roundly scolded for not paying attention to the time," Uncle Doll said.

No one answered him.

"It was windy," Bobby continued, "and Nanny looked like she was about to fall off the net."

"Off the *net*?" said Tiffany. "What net?"

"I was coming to that part. After you left," Bobby said, turning to the members of Team Starboard, "the boom began to swing around. Nanny was headed toward a net. It was suspended above the deck, and she was able to leap off the cable and grab on to it. But she'd gotten tangled up."

"It was better than being tangled in the moving cable, though," said Nanny.

Otto grinned and glanced at Johnny. "Now comes the good part," he said.

"Johnny handed me his cape, and he climbed up the net to Nanny," Bobby continued.

"The sailors were gone by then," added Nanny.

"The rest of us," said Bobby, "spread out Johnny's cape to make a landing net, like firefighters do. Johnny untangled Nanny . . ."

"And," said Nanny, "I shut my eyes and jumped."

"And we caught her!" exclaimed Mama Doll, sounding amazed.

"She landed smack in the center of our net," added Papa.

"Then Johnny climbed down to the deck and wrapped Nanny in his cape," said Bobby, "and we came back here."

"Goodness me," murmured Uncle Doll, wide-eyed.

"But what about the rest of the story?" Annabelle said to Nanny. "What happened when you first fell out of the box?"

Nanny rearranged her torn dress and said primly, "When I flew through the hole, the deck of *The Brown Pelican* was just below me, but instead of falling down, I shot through the air over the ship, and the next thing I knew I had sailed into the cable on the crane. I clung on for dear life. I thought I was lucky. If I had landed on the deck, well . . ." Nanny shivered. "For a long time," she went on, "the crane loaded pallets from the dock onto the ship, but I held on tight. I felt safe until I got stuck. And then the sailors came along and . . . well, thank goodness you found me," she said, looking at the members of Team Starboard.

"Nanny," said Annabelle hesitantly, "after you fell out of the box, did you by any chance see what happened to Bailey and Dad Funcraft?" And then a horrible thought occurred to her. "You do know they're missing, don't you?"

Nanny lowered her eyes. "Yes. I know. We were talking about it on the way back here. I saw them just after I grabbed on to the cable. The good news is that Mr. Funcraft is definitely on the ship."

"And Bailey?" whispered Mom Funcraft.

Nanny shook her head. "I don't know. I think he's on the ship, but I don't know where."

Tiffany rose to her feet, quivering. "Where did my father land?"

"One deck below the wheelhouse," replied Nanny. "I could tell you exactly where, but it won't make a difference."

"Why on earth not?" asked Mom Funcraft.

Nanny sighed. "When Bailey shot out of the hole, your husband was holding on to his feet. They dropped down faster than I did, I suppose because they weighed more. But your husband lost his grip before they landed. As I said, he wound up on the deck below the wheelhouse. On the port side," added Nanny, looking pleased with her nautical knowledge. "I didn't see where Bailey landed, although I don't think he could have flown clear across the ship, which is why he's probably on board. Somewhere."

"But why doesn't it matter that you saw where Mr. Funcraft landed?" asked Annabelle.

"I'm getting to that." Nanny began to look uncomfortable. "I had a good view of the ship from up on the crane, and I learned a few things. There are two children on board. There are no passengers on *The Brown Pelican* because it's a cargo ship, but the children are the daughter and son of the first mate, Myles Peachy the Second," Nanny explained. "The girl's name is Sasha. She's about eight. And her brother, Myles Peachy the Third, is six or so. They happened to be running along the deck just as Mr. Funcraft and Bailey sailed overhead. Sasha was carrying a little sailor doll and talking to her, so she didn't see the Funcrafts. But Mr. Funcraft dropped down in front of Myles, and Myles started shouting that this was the action doll he'd been wishing for. He was very excited. He believes that Mr. Funcraft can actually fly.

"He scooped him up," Nanny went on, "and showed him to Sasha—who thinks, as far as I can tell, that the doll must have been left behind by someone. At any rate, she isn't suspicious about where Mr. Funcraft came from. She even untied a scarf from around her doll's neck and gave it to Myles to use as a cape for his new doll."

"Just like Johnny's cape!" said Otto.

"Then Myles gave Mr. Funcraft a new name—Action Man—and he and Sasha walked off," Nanny finished up. "So Mr. Funcraft could be anywhere, you see."

"Huh," said Mom.

"That's quite a pickle!" yelled Tarquinius from the chalet.

"I'll say," agreed Tiffany. "How are we going to get Dad away from a boy? Especially a boy who wants an action doll as much as Myles does?"

"We'll find a way to rescue him," said Auntie Sarah.

"But we'd be stealing him from a little boy," said Annabelle.

"There's nothing in the Doll Code of Honor about not stealing dolls," Freya pointed out.

"It's not honorable to steal. Period," said Mama.

Tiffany frowned. "But he's Nora Palmer's doll, not Myles Peachy's. We have to make things right."

"Not by stealing," said Papa.

"But it's *not* stealing. It's returning him to his rightful owner—and to his family," snapped Tiffany.

Annabelle glanced up then as she heard a door bang on the far side of the hold.

"Shh," said Auntie Sarah. "Someone's down here. It's another day. The ship is waking up. We're going to have to wait until dark to do anything about Mr. Funcraft."

Nanny shook her head. "I think Myles took Mr. Funcraft to bed with him last night. And I believe the children sleep with the door to their room shut. If you want to find Mr. Funcraft, I think you'll have to search for him during the day when Myles will be out playing with his new toy."

"All right," said Auntie Sarah eventually. "I guess we don't have any choice but to risk a daytime Exploration."

CHAPTER TEN

Sassafras

AN HOUR LATER the three teams set out again, leaving Nanny behind to recuperate on a bed of tissue paper. Annabelle found that she was far more nervous on this Exploration than she had been on either of the first two. It was now broad daylight, and just as Auntie Sarah had predicted, the ship was a very busy place. In the hold alone, the members of Team Starboard twice had to dodge between pallets to escape the feet (and the eyes) of sailors.

"My land," whispered Auntie Sarah the second time this happened.

"People seem to come out of nowhere," said Mom Funcraft.

"What do you think a sailor would do if he saw us?" asked Tiffany, and Annabelle studied her friend. This was the kind of question *Annabelle* usually asked.

"Better not to find out," Auntie Sarah replied.

The dolls peeked cautiously around a carton labeled BARKY'S ORGANIC DOG TREATS—HEALTHY TREATS FOR HEALTHY DOGS!

"Are they gone?" whispered Tiffany.

"I think so," said her mother.

The dolls listened for footsteps from the safety of their hiding place.

"How on earth are we going to walk around on the upper decks?" asked Mom. "There will be people everywhere."

Auntie Sarah sighed. "It will be dangerous, but I don't know how else to locate Mr. Funcraft. We have to hope we'll come across Myles Peachy playing with him. Come along, everyone. Annabelle, make good mental notes. We'll move slowly and cautiously. Be prepared to hide again at a moment's notice."

The dolls didn't encounter anyone on

the ramp leading out of the hold, and they made their way unnoticed up to the next level as well. But by the time they'd reached the deck where Nanny had said Dad Funcraft had landed, they'd had to jump out of sight no fewer than six times. They had tumbled behind a coiled rope, between a pair of boots, under a tarpaulin, and behind a life raft, and twice they had simply darted around a corner, hoping they wouldn't run into anyone on the other side.

"This is nerve-racking!" exclaimed Mom Funcraft after they had hidden for a seventh time. The dolls were huddled under a cap that had blown off of someone's head.

"How are we going to have a proper search when we have to keep stopping to hide?" asked Annabelle.

"I don't think we *are* going to have a proper search," replied Tiffany, "but we have to look anyway." Then, wrinkling her nose and looking disapprovingly at the underside of the cap, she added, "It smells in here."

"We should at least find our way to the children's room so we know where it is," said Mom Funcraft. "Maybe Myles Peachy the Third will leave my husband there at some point—with the door open. He can't carry him around *all* day."

The dolls peered out from beneath the hat.

"The coast is clear," whispered Tiffany. "I think."

"Let me check," said Annabelle. But no sooner had she crept onto the deck again than she heard footsteps and darted back inside. "Two people are coming," she reported. "We can't leave yet."

"This isn't working," said Tiffany, holding her nose. "We need a better plan. Let's go back to our box. I'll bet the other teams are going back too."

Auntie Sarah let out a long sigh. "All right. Does everyone agree with Tiffany?"

"Yes," said Annabelle and Mom reluctantly.

The dolls set forth again. They had walked no more than ten feet when Annabelle suddenly pulled the others behind the same coiled rope that had hidden them earlier. "Did you see what I just saw?" she whispered.

"No. What?" asked Mom.

"Sasha. The girl. It must have been her. She's about Kate's age. And she was carrying a sailor doll."

"Where?" asked Tiffany stepping away from the rope. "Oh, I see her. There she is!"

"Follow her!" whispered Auntie Sarah. "We have to talk to her doll. She'll be able to help us."

Yes! Dolls always stick together, Annabelle thought, just as Tiffany said, "*If* she's a living doll."

"She has to be," Annabelle replied, puffing along after Sasha, who walked about fifty times faster than any of the members of Team Starboard.

Annabelle breathed a sigh of relief when Sasha came to a stop. She watched as she settled the doll under a deck chair where she wouldn't be stepped on by hustling sailors, pulled a pair of binoculars out of her pocket, and began to walk alongside the ship's railing, the binoculars trained on the ocean.

The members of Team Starboard huddled behind a deck cushion and studied the doll.

"Maybe we could give her a message to take to your husband," Auntie Sarah said to Mom.

"We can't do anything until we find out whether she's a living doll," Annabelle pointed out.

Sasha was now a good distance away. This little corner of the ship seemed quiet. Annabelle, Tiffany, Auntie Sarah, and Mom crept forward until they were standing under the chair just inches from the doll.

She was bigger than Baby Betsy, Annabelle noted, with dark brown eyes, a smile on her lips, and real hair, soft and curly. The blue-and-white sailor suit she wore was pressed and clean, and on her feet were shiny black Mary Jane shoes.

The doll looked sweet. But she didn't move a muscle when Team Starboard approached; she just sat stiffly, leaning against a chair leg and staring vacantly at her hands.

Annabelle caught Tiffany's eye. She glanced at the doll and then at Tiffany again and shrugged. Finally Annabelle screwed up her courage, tugged on the doll's sleeve, and whispered, "Are you alive?"

The doll blinked her eyes and sat up straighter. She opened her mouth. "Shiver me timbers!" she said loudly. "Shake a leg! Tell it to the Marines."

Annabelle gasped—and prepared to run.

But from farther down the deck, not taking her eyes off the ocean, Sasha merely called, "Oh, Sassafras. There you go again. When we get to England maybe Pop can have you fixed. I'm going to ask him about that right now." She scurried down a flight of stairs.

Annabelle tried to calm her pounding heart. "That was close," she said, and sank to the deck.

But Tiffany remained standing. "Your name is Sassafras?" she asked the sailor doll.

The doll nodded. "Shipshape and Bristol fashion!"

The members of Team Starboard frowned at one another.

"Excuse me?" said Mom Funcraft.

"Batten down the hatches! Anchors aweigh!" Sassafras jumped to her feet.

"Is *The Brown Pelican* headed for *England*?" asked Annabelle.

"On your beam ends!"

"Do you speak English?" asked Tiffany.

"That *is* English," replied Annabelle. "It just doesn't make any sense."

Tiffany gaped at Sassafras, who was now

pacing excitedly in the shade below the chair. "What's wrong with her?" she blurted out.

"Tiffany! Mind your manners," said Mom Funcraft. She pulled Tiffany aside and Annabelle heard her say, "It's rude to talk about someone when she's right in front of you."

Annabelle decided to give Sassafras one more try. "Hi," she said. "My name is Annabelle, and I'm a living doll. What's your name?"

"Between the devil and the deep blue sea!"

Annabelle sighed. She stepped away from Sassafras and waved the others back to the deck cushion. "What *is* wrong with her?" she asked quietly.

Auntie Sarah shook her head. "I don't know. Whatever it is, I hope Sasha can have her fixed when we get to England. I'm afraid Sassafras isn't going to be any help to us, though."

Annabelle looked balefully at her aunt. "That's another thing. We're going to England. *England*," she moaned. "How are we ever going to get back to Kate and Nora?"

"I don't know," Auntie Sarah said again. "But first things first. It's imperative that we find Bailey and Mr. Funcraft. If we're going on such a long journey, then we must go to together."

It was a sad group of explorers that made its way back to the pallet in the hold. Team Starboard's foray had taken hours, and they had found nothing but a broken doll and learned that they were to travel more than three thousand miles from their home. When at last they crawled through the hole and into their box, they found that Team Port and Team Merdoll had already returned.

"Anybody have any luck?" asked Mom Funcraft glumly.

"Not much," Papa Doll replied. "It's awfully difficult to search during the daytime."

The dolls agreed that they would postpone further searching until that evening.

"We might have learned one thing, though," said Bobby. "We think we found Myles and Sasha's room. But we aren't sure."

"The door was closed," added Papa.

"Oh," said Tiffany, disappointed. "We were hoping the door would be open during the day. How are we ever going to get in there?"

No one had an answer.

"We found a shoe," said Freya. "That's all anybody seems to find. Shoes." She held up a chunky block of yellow plastic.

"That's Bailey's!" cried Mom, grabbing for it. She held the shoe to her cheek and murmured, "Out there somewhere without his shoe."

"Where was it?" Annabelle wanted to know.

"Near something called . . . What did we hear that sailor say?" Freya asked Neptune.

"The deckhouse."

"Near the deckhouse."

"Hmm," said Bobby. "But I suppose it doesn't mean much. Bailey could still be any-where."

"We found out that the ship is sailing for England," said Annabelle. "All the way to England."

"I'm not surprised!" bellowed Tarquinius. "Makes sense!"

"*And* we found Sasha's sailor doll," added Tiffany. She told the others about their encounter with Sassafras, adding, "All she says are these weird things like 'Batten down the hatches' and 'Shiver me timbers.'"

Bobby looked thoughtful. "Huh."

Giselle's voice floated up from the carton below. "I remember once when all I could say was *bonjour*. Over and over and over again. Remember that, Quinnie? *Bonjour! Bonjour! Bonjour!*"

"Oh, stop! Of course I remember. Darned annoying it was. I kept talking to you, and all you would say was . . . that word. Nearly drove me crazy."

"How did you cure yourself?" Bobby called to Giselle.

"Cure myself? Why, *rien*. I did nothing."

"It went on for days," said Tarquinius. "Very strange. At times it seemed as if we were having a real conversation. Giselle could use . . . that word . . . in many different ways. She has a very expressive voice, in case you haven't noticed. Finally one day I made a rather silly joke and I slapped her on the back, and she said, 'Don't be ridiculous,' and that was that. The episode was over."

"But don't you see?" cried Bobby. "Her talking mechanism must have been stuck, and when you slapped her on the back, you unstuck it. You do have a talking mechanism, don't you, Giselle?"

"*Mais oui.* I do. It hasn't been activated in years, but I have one."

"Then that's our answer," Bobby said triumphantly. "Sassafras must have one too. And since she's a sailor doll, she's been programmed to say nautical things. If we can fix the mechanism, maybe she could help us after all."

Auntie Sarah clapped her hands together. "Excellent!" she said. "That will be our next mission."

"Doll power!" cried Annabelle, suddenly feeling hopeful.

And Tarquinius bellowed, "You will all head out tonight with renewed vigor!"

CHAPTER ELEVEN

Midnight Search

THE DOLLS DID indeed begin their next search with renewed vigor—after enduring a wait for midnight that seemed endless. Annabelle and Tiffany and some of the merdolls crawled into the box below to keep Giselle and Tarquinius company. The merdolls told stories, and Giselle taught everyone to say "I am very bored" in French. But nothing relieved Annabelle's boredom or Tiffany's anxiety, and both girls were cranky by the time the bell clanged for the midnight watch.

"All right, Team Starboard," said Auntie Sarah. "Our mission tonight is to try to find either Sassafras or Mr. Funcraft. The other teams are going to look for Bailey. That's a bigger job, since we have no idea where he is."

"Who do we start with?" asked Tiffany. "My father or Sassafras?"

"Let's just see what happens when we reach the upper deck. We'll look for the cabin where Bobby thinks the children's berths are. But keep your eyes open, because we could come across Sassafras anywhere. And no dawdling!" said Auntie Sarah briskly. "We don't have much time."

"Speaking of dawdling," said Mom

Funcraft as the dolls made their way down the pallet, "Tiffany and Annabelle, you need to stay close to Sarah and me. Sometimes you lagged behind."

"We're looking for another porp—" Annabelle started to say, but Tiffany clapped her hand over her mouth.

"It's important that we stick together," said Mom firmly. "The last thing we need is another missing doll person."

"Besides, we're on a mission," Auntie Sarah reminded them.

"Keep your eyes on the prize," added Mom.

Annabelle did not like to be scolded, and she climbed sullenly down to the floor of the hold and remained silent as the dolls made their way to the ramp. But she took Tiffany's hand and made an effort to stay closer to the grown-ups.

This time the trip to the upper deck went much more quickly. The dolls still huffed and puffed and chugged, but they knew where they were going, and unlike the hectic daytime Exploration, the midnight search was quiet and they encountered only two people.

"I think," whispered Mom Funcraft, "that it was right around here that we met Sasha and Sassafras. Does anyone see the chair—"

Mom abruptly stopped speaking. A loud grinding seemed to cause the very air to vibrate, and Annabelle could feel the ship start to slow down.

"What on earth?" murmured Auntie Sarah.

"We couldn't possibly have reached England already. Could we?" asked Mom Funcraft.

"We haven't found Dad or Bailey yet!" cried Tiffany with a sob.

And the merdolls haven't been set free, thought Annabelle, but she had the good sense not to say that aloud and concentrated instead on comforting Tiffany.

Auntie Sarah shook her head. "Calm down, calm down. We haven't even been gone for a day and a half yet."

"But why are we stopping?" asked Annabelle. "In the middle of the ocean and the middle of the night?"

"I have no idea," said Auntie Sarah, and then suddenly looked over her shoulder.

"Hide!" she hissed. "Everyone—behind that bucket!"

The four dolls skittered behind a plastic bucket just as several pairs of booted feet tromped past them. Moments later Annabelle watched in awe as sailors began to let down the ship's anchors.

"Tell me again why we're stopping here," Annabelle heard one ask another.

"It's the captain. He works with NOAA sometimes."

"Noah?"

"No, NOAA. The National Oceanic and Atmospheric Administration. They study the weather, chart the seas and skies, and help protect the ocean. Captain Brown takes water samples for them on our routes. We have to stay here tonight to take another sample from the same spot tomorrow morning."

The first sailor shrugged his shoulders. "How many times will we have to stop for this? It makes the trip take longer."

"Just one more time, on the other side of the Atlantic. Off the Scilly Isles."

Annabelle couldn't help herself. She nudged Auntie Sarah. "That gives us more time to search for the Funcrafts," she whispered, and she felt some of her crabbiness creep away.

She watched as a man wearing a snappy white uniform and a white cap appeared and lowered a beaker over the side of the ship and down toward the water. The captain, she thought. That must be Captain Brown.

The dolls waited until the water sample had been collected and the sailors and Captain Brown had moved on, leaving the anchors in place.

"All right," said Mom Funcraft when the deck had been quiet for several minutes. "Let's look for the chair Sassafras was sitting under when we met her this morning."

"She won't be there *now*," said Tiffany. "Sasha probably took her to bed with her."

But Tiffany was wrong. Auntie Sarah spotted the chair, and there was Sassafras sitting placidly beneath it, feet crossed daintily at the ankles.

"You're still here!" cried Annabelle as the dolls crowded around her. "We were hoping we'd find you."

"Full to the gunwales!" exclaimed Sassafras.

Annabelle glanced at her aunt.

Auntie Sarah said patiently, "Sassafras, I know you don't know us, but we need your help."

"Walk the plank! Walk the plank!"

"Psssst! Annabelle!"

Annabelle jumped as a voice whispered against the back of her neck and a hand grabbed her shoulder. She spun around. "Bobby! What are you doing here? You nearly gave me a heart attack." She saw the rest of Team Port hustling to catch up with her brother.

"Sorry. I'm sorry, Annabelle. I didn't mean to scare you," said Bobby. "We were searching up here and we saw you talking with Sassafras. I thought we should meet her."

Team Starboard stepped aside as Bobby leaned in for a closer look at the sailor doll. He stuck out his hand. "My name is Bobby. Pleased to meet you."

"Go by the board!" exclaimed Sassafras.

"I wish her voice weren't so loud," Annabelle whispered to Tiffany.

Bobby frowned at Sassafras. Then he said, "I have an idea. Let's see if you can follow instructions. If you can, then we'll know you understand what we're saying." He paused, thinking. Finally he said, "Sassafras, if you're a true living doll and you've taken the oath, stand up."

Nine pairs of eyes fixed themselves on Sassafras. For a moment she remained sitting on the deck. Then, very slowly, she uncrossed her ankles and got to her feet. She stood up, teetering slightly, and offered a smile to the dolls.

"Ah! Wonderful!" cried Auntie Sarah. "Now sit down again." When Sassafras was seated once more, Auntie Sarah whacked her on the back.

Sassafras emitted a small "ugh."

So Bobby stepped forward and clapped Sassafras on the back.

"Ugh!" she said more loudly.

"My turn!" cried Tiffany, sounding suddenly cheerful, and she too whonked Sassafras on the back.

"*Ugh!* That's—"

Annabelle couldn't help herself. She slapped Sassafras, and the sailor doll tumbled forward.

"OW!" she cried. She rubbed the spot between her shoulder blades where everyone had whapped her. "Shiver my timbers! Are you trying to kill me?" She got to her feet.

"I'm sorry," exclaimed Auntie Sarah. "We didn't mean to hurt—"

But Bobby interrupted her. "What did you just say?" he asked, looking up at Sassafras.

"I *said*," said Sassafras, "are you trying

179

to—" She put her hand to her mouth. "Oh! I can speak again!"

Bobby grinned. "So I was right. Your talking mechanism was stuck." He turned to the others. "Just like Giselle's. A good whack on the back was all she needed."

Everyone began talking at once, and the dolls had so many questions for the sailor doll that finally Auntie Sarah called, "Stop, stop! Calm down. We're making an awful lot of noise. And I think we're frightening Sassafras. Just let her tell us her story in her own way."

So Sassafras, who did indeed look overwhelmed, sat down again, and the dolls sat around her in a semicircle. "Well," said Sassafras, "after I took the oath in the toy factory, I was shipped to a department store in London, and that's where Sasha's father bought me. I've been with Sasha and her family ever since. Sasha and Myles live here on the boat with their father. They travel all around the world. They even do their lessons on the boat. Sasha is a wonderful friend and she takes good care of me . . . um, except sometimes she forgets and leaves me behind. Like right now. But she'll come find me soon. She always does. And Myles is . . ." Sassafras paused for a long time before she continued. "Myles is a very nice boy, but he plays rough, and he's the one who broke my speaking apparatus. He pulled the cord so many times that finally it snapped off. I'm glad I can talk to you now, but I'll still have to go to a doll hospital in London because Sasha wants to have the cord fixed," she finished up. She took a gulp of air.

"Now," she went on, "tell me who you are and how you wound up on the boat. Where did you come from?"

Annabelle told Sassafras their story, with the others jumping in from time to time to add details. "So you see," Annabelle said at last, "we really need to get Tiffany's father back from Sasha's brother. We don't want to make Myles sad—"

"But it's my fault Dad is missing!" Tiffany blurted out. "We have to get him back. We love him."

"You'll get him back," said Sassafras. "I know you will. I'll help you in whatever way I can."

"Thank you," Tiffany replied humbly.

The dolls talked and talked. The members of Team Port and Team Starboard asked Sassafras questions about Myles and Sasha and their habits and whether the door to the children's cabin was always closed. By the time the sky was starting to lighten, they had no firm plans for a rescue but plenty more information—enough so that they could return to their pallet and begin plotting.

At last Annabelle peeked out from under the chair and realized that the sun was starting to rise, turning the horizon a bright pink. This was when she heard a sleepy voice.

"Oh, Sassafras," said Sasha, "did I leave you out here again?"

"Run!" cried Sassafras, and nine tiny dolls scattered and hid behind buckets and boots, under hats and in coils of rope, just as a pair of bare feet strode to the chair and a hand reached down to scoop up the sailor doll.

"Thank goodness," said Sasha softly. "I'm so sorry. I'll put you to bed right now."

Annabelle didn't turn around to watch.

"Time to go," whispered Mom Funcraft. "On the double. The ship will be waking up."

But the dolls didn't have a chance to move. The deck suddenly became a flurry of activity again as two sailors and Captain Brown reappeared, and the captain took another water sample. Not until the sailors were going about their usual business again did the dolls dare to scurry away, Annabelle and Tiffany at the back of the group.

Tiffany looked ahead at the rest of the search teams, and then at Annabelle. "Come on," she said. "Mom wants us to keep up, remember?"

"But isn't the sunrise lovely?" said Annabelle breathily, pausing to look at the sky.

"Beautiful," agreed Tiffany. "Now come on." She tugged at Annabelle's sleeve.

"Uh-oh, look!" Annabelle pointed to a large gray-and-white bird as it swooped down from its perch on a railing and planted itself in front of the girls. They froze—and the rest of the members of Team Starboard and Team Port continued on their way.

Seagull, thought Annabelle. I'm face-to-face with a seagull. Well, face-to-leg. And this bird is as big as a cat. Annabelle looked up, up, up to the seagull's head. She couldn't take her painted eyes off the bird's beady ones. She felt hypnotized. The seagull could snatch her up in its mouth in two seconds, but Annabelle was too afraid to run.

"In here!" squeaked Tiffany from nearby, and she grabbed Annabelle's hand and pulled her backward, jerking her away from the seagull. She shoved her friend into a dank, dark hole in the deck, into which a heavy chain was threaded, and jumped in after her. Annabelle slipped and slid downward,

the way she had once seen Nora go flying feetfirst down a playground slide. She felt around wildly for something that would stop her fall, and her hands grasped a link of the smooth, cold chain. She wrapped her arms around it. Below her feet she thought she could see daylight, and she hugged the chain more tightly.

"What is this place?" whispered Annabelle hoarsely, feet dangling.

Her arms ached, but she didn't dare let go of the chain.

"Don't look down," said Tiffany breathlessly, and only then did Annabelle realize that Tiffany's feet were planted firmly on her head. "Remember when Bobby was telling us all that stuff about the ship?" said Tiffany. "I think this is what he said is called the hawse pipe, and I'm pretty sure the anchor is attached to the other end of this chain. See? The chain goes out the bottom of the pipe and down the side of the ship into the ocean. And—"

"And," Annabelle interrupted her

friend, "we're going to set sail again pretty soon, which means the anchor is going to get hauled back up."

"Oh," said Tiffany. "Yeah. We have to get out of here."

"Right now. So climb," Annabelle ordered her friend. "Climb back up the chain and I'll follow you."

"Okay, but this isn't going to be easy." Tiffany grunted and groaned.

Annabelle waited until she felt Tiffany step off her head, and then she began to hoist herself up through the hole, hands slipping, feet scrabbling. She was halfway back to the deck when her awful sweater snagged on something sharp. Annabelle tugged at the sweater. She couldn't free it. She tugged some more, and suddenly she felt the sweater go slack as the yarn began to unravel.

Annabelle lost her grip on the chain and fell backward.

Down,

down,

down.

Far above her she heard a terrified scream from Tiffany. "Annabelle!"

CHAPTER TWELVE

Down the Hawse Pipe

ANNABELLE COULDN'T STOP herself, couldn't grab the chain. As the sweater continued to unravel, she tumbled head over heels, facing first the ocean, then the sky, then the side of the ship, then the ocean again, as she bounced off the links of the chain. And the ocean was growing closer. What would happen when she hit the water? Would she float? But where would she float to? The ship would soon be on its way again, and Annabelle would be left behind. What would become of a tiny doll alone in the vast, vast ocean?

Perhaps a friendly fish would come along and . . .

And what? Even a friendly fish would probably think Annabelle was a meal and would swallow her up gratefully. Annabelle tried to recall the story of Jonah and the whale that Grandma Katherine had told to Kate and Nora. Maybe Annabelle would fall into the mouth of a whale. Surely she would be able to survive in such a vast space. But gurgling around inside a whale's stomach wasn't a very appealing idea, and anyway the whale might travel for hundreds of miles and Annabelle would wind up far from her family and friends.

The sweater continued to unravel.

Annabelle continued to fall.

Perhaps, she thought, she would be rescued once she reached the ocean. After all, Tiffany knew what had happened to her. But who on *The Brown Pelican* would bother to jump overboard to rescue a tiny doll that didn't belong to anyone on the ship?

No one, that was who.

The sky appeared above Annabelle's head again, and then a length of chain flashed by.

Annabelle hoped the water landing would be soft. And then she remembered a horrible fact that Bobby had proudly reported to her one night after he had spent an evening secretly watching the Palmers' television. "Did you know," he had said, "that falling onto water from a great height is just like falling onto cement?"

Annabelle let out a shriek as the water rose to meet her.

She closed her eyes.

Like falling onto cement. Her china body falling onto cement.

She pictured her house in the corner of Kate's room, and her bed in the nursery. She thought of Mama's gentle face as she sat with Annabelle in the quiet time after the Palmers had gone to sleep, when they talked about bravery and dollkind. She thought about Papa and Auntie Sarah and Uncle Doll and Nanny and her brother and her sisters.

And suddenly she wasn't falling anymore.

She had stopped with a silent jerk. The unraveling yarn had reached a knot that Kate had made near the top of one sleeve, and Annabelle was dangling in the air. The ocean was still far below her. She looked upward. The opening of the hawse pipe was above her, although not as far above her as she had thought it would be.

Holding tightly to the yarn with one hand, Annabelle reached for the chain with her free hand.

From somewhere aboard *The Brown Pelican*, she heard a voice call, "Weigh anchor!"

CHAPTER THIRTEEN

Up the Hawse Pipe

ANNABELLE WASN'T CERTAIN what, precisely, "Weigh anchor" meant, but she had an idea that the anchor that was attached to the chain she was grasping would soon begin to make its ponderous way up out of the ocean.

Maybe I could get a free ride on the chain, she thought, before she realized that the length of yarn from which she was dangling would almost certainly get tangled in the massive links of the chain as it was cranked upward. Not to mention that even if she did somehow manage to ride back to the deck unharmed, there was a good chance that she would be noticed by at least one human when she arrived.

Annabelle didn't have time to thank her lucky stars that Kate was such a horrible knitter that she had made a big sloppy knot in the sweater, which had stopped the unraveling and prevented Annabelle from falling any farther. She couldn't think about the fact that she had not smashed onto the water like glass onto pavement, or that she was not slopping around inside the stomach of a whale. All Annabelle could do was let out a quiet cry of "Doll power!" and then start the climb back to the opening of the hawse pipe—moving as fast as she was able.

At first she let go of the yarn and tried shinnying her way up the chain, but almost immediately the yarn got tangled in the links, which were oily and slippery and almost impossible to hold on to anyway. Annabelle tipped her head back and looked up, straining to see the machine that would haul the anchor out of the water. (What had Bobby said this machine was called? The windlass?) She couldn't see it, but she could

hear activity somewhere above her.

Hurry, Annabelle said to herself. You have to hurry. You have to find a way to reach the top before the chain begins to move. With the ocean far below her, her hands shaking, Annabelle dared to let go of the chain and reach for the yarn again. She gripped it with both hands and began to pull herself

up,

up,

up,

pushing off from the links with her feet, just the way she climbed the strips of plastic on the pallet in the hold.

In this way Annabelle made her way toward the hawse pipe much more quickly than she could have imagined. She found herself climbing in a rhythm: pushing off, then reaching hand over hand. Push, reach, reach. Push, reach, reach. Push, reach, reach.

Her mind began to wander. And as sometimes happened when she was daydreaming, a wonderful thought suddenly sprang to life. Now that Annabelle knew about the anchor chain and the hawse pipe, and now that she knew it was possible to climb up—and presumably down—the chain, why couldn't she suggest to the merdolls that they use the chain as a ladder into the sea? If Captain Brown was going to drop anchor again in the Scilly Isles, near the end of the trip, then maybe the merdolls could plan to lower themselves down the chain and slip into the ocean there.

Push, reach, reach. Push, reach, reach.

Annabelle was nearing the top of the chain. She climbed more confidently now, pleased both with her skill and with her idea for the merdolls. She paused to listen for voices, but heard only creaks and groans from the ship and gentle splashes from the ocean. "Tiffany?" she called softly. "Tiffany?" She longed to see her friend poke her head through the opening of the hawse pipe, but realized that by this time Tiffany had probably made her way back up to the deck and gone for help.

Annabelle wanted to stop, to pause with her feet on a link of the chain and rest her aching muscles and sore hands. How long ago had she heard the call of "Weigh anchor"? She wasn't sure, but she knew she couldn't waste a single second.

Push, reach, reach. Push, reach, reach.

Just when Annabelle was certain that her legs were about to give out, she realized that she was no longer staring at the side of the ship. Instead she was looking into the Hawse pipe. She pumped her fist in the air. "I did it!" she whispered.

Annabelle continued inching along the yarn until she came to the spot where it had snagged. Then she paused only long enough to wrench the yarn free and pull the rest of it up after her—thinking as she did so how pleased Mama and Papa would be to hear that she had left no trace of her adventure behind for the humans to find—before finishing her journey and emerging onto the deck.

She didn't stop for a second, not even

to look for the seagull. She simply picked up her feet and ran. When she heard voices, she ducked behind a post, cradling her armful of dirty yarn. She waited until she had also heard the motor of the windlass grind to life, and then she started moving again as, behind her, the anchor was slowly heaved up out of the water, the chain winding noisily around the wheel. Annabelle ran, and didn't stop running until she found a quiet spot on the deck. Then she slumped to the floor and sat, knees drawn to her chest, until her breathing had slowed and her legs had stopped shaking.

Annabelle wasn't sure when she fell asleep, but she awakened with a jerk when she heard a voice call, "Look! Over there!"

Annabelle was on her feet in an instant, her head swiveling from side to side as she searched for a hiding place. She didn't see one, so she began to run.

"Wait! Annabelle! It's us!"

Annabelle whirled around. The members of Team Starboard were running toward

her. She dropped her armload of yarn and collapsed onto it while Auntie Sarah gathered her into a hug.

"I can't believe we found you!" exclaimed Mom Funcraft. "How on earth did you get back? Tiffany told us what happened."

Auntie Sarah now held Annabelle away from her and eyed her rather severely. "We didn't know where the two of you had gone," she said. "Mrs. Funcraft and I had to search for you in broad daylight."

"I'm sorry." Annabelle thought Auntie Sarah had more to say, but Tiffany was jumping up and down, wringing her hands.

"How on earth did you get back up here, Annabelle?" she cried. "Did you fall in the ocean? Did you have to swim? Are you hurt?" Finally she stepped away and took a good look at her friend. "What happened to your sweater?" she asked.

Annabelle glanced down at the remains of her sweater, which was now not much more than a collar of yarn. "It unraveled," she said. And she told Team Starboard how she had fallen and how she had rescued herself.

Tiffany listened, her gaze fixed admiringly on Annabelle. "You did all that? By yourself? You—you're so brave, Annabelle."

Annabelle was about to say, *Me? Brave?* but at that moment Auntie Sarah said, "Very resourceful of you."

"And you didn't leave any traces behind," added Mom Funcraft. "Impressive."

"However," said Auntie Sarah, "this could have had a very bad ending, Annabelle. I'm trying hard not to say 'I told you so,' but have you learned your lesson?"

"Oh, yes!"

"Yes," added Tiffany emphatically. "We

have definitely learned our lesson. We'll stick with the team from now on."

Auntie Sarah glanced around the ship's deck. "All right. It's time to go back to our box. We were willing to risk a daytime Exploration after your, um, unfortunate mishap, but we'd better hide ourselves now. And we should rest. We'll have a lot to do tonight."

The members of Team Starboard began to wind their way back to the pallet. They moved quickly and quietly, but when they reached the hold and found it silent—no signs of humans—Annabelle felt it was safe to speak. "I have a question," she said. "If we ever get back home again, what will the Palmers think has happened to us? They'll see my sweater and they'll see how dirty we are and"—Annabelle tactfully refrained from mentioning the missing dolls—"well, aren't we putting dollkind at risk?"

"I don't think so," Auntie Sarah replied thoughtfully. "After all, none of this was our fault. The Palmers mixed up our box. If we do get home, and if they learn the truth about what happened to us, they'll think we had a very rough voyage and they'll simply be glad to have us back."

"But my sweater," said Annabelle rue-fully. "How could a sweater unravel from a bad voyage? The Palmers are going to won-der. Not that I liked the sweater," she added quickly.

Auntie Sarah shook her head. "Not our problem. This isn't our concern because it wasn't our fault. You can stop worrying."

Tiffany managed a smile. "Just be glad that hideous thing is gone."

Annabelle walked a few more steps and then she said, "Something else. While I was climbing back up to the hawse pipe, I had an idea. A really good one. But I'm going to wait until we're all together before I tell you about it."

"Ooh," said Tiffany. "A mystery."

When Team Starboard reached the pallet, they found that the other search teams had already returned. The dolls talked quietly, everyone chattering about their adventures and, after they learned what had happened to Annabelle, hugging her and exclaiming over her.

"My poor baby," cried Mama, who

immediately burst into tears.

"I almost got stepped on by a sailor!" said Bobby, shuddering.

"What did you do to your sweater?" asked Johnny.

"*Ja*, it is a mess," said Otto.

"We saw a dolphin!" exclaimed Freya. "A real dolphin."

"Tell us all about your adventure, Annabelle," said Uncle Doll. "Don't leave anything out."

At last, with the members of all three teams crowded around Annabelle, she was able to tell her story. Her audience listened quietly, but every so often, from the box below, Tarquinius would bellow, "What was that? Speak up, missy! We want to hear every word!"

Annabelle finished her tale at last but immediately said, "And that's not all. While I was climbing back up to the ship, I had a great idea." She looked around at the faces that were eagerly looking back at hers.

"What is it?" asked Poseidon.

"I know," said Annabelle slowly, and her eyes settled on Freya, "how you can leave the ship and go safely into the ocean."

Freya drew in her breath. "You do?" she whispered.

"How?" asked Tiffany.

"Yes, how?" called Giselle.

"Down the hawse pipe," Annabelle replied. And she told them about her plan.

"A home at last in the Scilly Isles," murmured Freya. "They sound magical."

"They sound silly," said Seastar.

"We can get down the chain," said Neptune thoughtfully. "I know we can."

"We'll carry our tails with us and put them on just before we slip into the ocean," said Silver.

"We'll be at the Scilly Isles in a few days," Annabelle reminded her new friends.

"Just think," said Freya dreamily. "A few days and we'll be able to start work on our kingdom."

CHAPTER FOURTEEN

Johnny to the Rescue

THE MERDOLLS WERE so excited by the thought of starting their kingdom in the waters off the Scilly Isles that they couldn't stop talking. The ATC box hummed with vibrant merdoll voices—chattering and chanting and planning. At last Auntie Sarah stood up on the head of the stuffed kitten and made an announcement. "It is time for everyone in this box to take a rest. After that we need to plan Mr. Funcraft's rescue."

"Aren't we forgetting something?" asked Annabelle. "What about Bailey?"

"We haven't forgotten about him," said

Auntie Sarah patiently. "But we have no idea where he is. And we do know where Tiffany's father is. Or at least we know whom he's with. So let's concentrate on him for now. One doll at a time.

"To that end," Auntie Sarah continued, "we must have all our strength. Not to mention our wits. So as I was saying, we need to rest."

"This is naptime, *ja*?" said Otto.

"I don't need a nap!" exclaimed Johnny.

"There's no point in arguing with her," whispered Annabelle.

So the dolls rested. Nanny was made to lie down on her tissue paper bed again. The merdolls and Johnny and Otto returned to their own boxes for an hour. The others sat quietly except for Annabelle, who fell sound asleep and wakened much later to discover that everyone else was already up and that a meeting was underway.

"Why did you let me sleep?" she said crossly to Tiffany, who was sitting nearby, holding Seastar in her lap.

"Auntie Sarah said you were exhausted after your accidental adventure."

"Hmphh. Well, what's going on?"

"Just listen."

"What makes me nervous," Mom Funcraft was saying, "is that according to Sassafras, Myles Peachy tosses my husband up in the air a lot. It's some sort of game. He throws my husband around and then runs after him. What if he were to throw him down a pipe or up into a net? If that happens, we might not be able to rescue him before we arrive in England."

"Myles does seem awfully careless," agreed Nanny. "I saw that for myself."

"Maybe we could use his carelessness to our advantage," said Uncle Doll. "What if sometime when Mr. Funcraft is separated from Myles, he slips away? Myles would simply think he had lost his doll. Then we could sneak Mr. Funcraft back here."

"Actually, that might be a good lesson for Myles," said Mama. "It would teach him to be more responsible."

"I don't know," said Bobby. "Myles is so happy with his Action Man. It seems mean to take his doll away from him. He doesn't know Mr. Funcraft belongs to someone else."

Mom Funcraft scowled. "He is my

husband," she said fiercely. "We have to rescue him. We have to."

"Of course we do," Auntie Sarah replied
soothingly.

An uncomfortable silence settled over
the box. Then Johnny stood up. He cleared
his throat. "Ahem. I have an idea," he said,
looking shyly around at all the pairs of eyes
that were trained on him. "I agree that it isn't
right to steal from a boy, especially from a boy
who hasn't done anything wrong. We don't
want to make him sad. But what if someone
were to take Mr. Funcraft's place?"

"What do you mean?" asked Tiffany.

Johnny cleared his throat again. "I
haven't belonged to anybody for a long time
now," he said. "Not for years. I've just been
lying around in boxes or attics, waiting." He
paused. "Waiting and waiting. It's no fun.
And it's lonely. Nobody even wanted to buy
me at the yard sale."

Annabelle watched Otto, who was sitting
at Johnny's feet. His eyes had grown large as
he'd listened to his new friend. Now they glis-
tened with tears. But he said nothing.

From below, Tarquinius shouted,

"What's your point, Superman?"

"My point is that I need a human who will play with me. I miss action and adventure and games. I want a boy or a girl who will fly me around a room and make me rescue people from a burning building. Or stick me in an ambulance and zoom me across the floor to a pileup of Matchbox cars. I want . . . I want to be Myles's Action Man."

"Do you mean," said Tiffany, "that you could take my father's place?"

Johnny nodded.

Annabelle saw a tear slip down Otto's cheek.

Mama and Papa exchanged glances.

"I say!" boomed Tarquinius. "That's a brilliant idea! Simply brilliant."

"Ah," said Giselle more quietly. "You are a true superhero, Johnny. You have solved the problem neatly."

"That's a very generous offer," said Nanny.

"But wait a minute. Let's think this over carefully," spoke up Uncle Doll. "If we switched Johnny for Mr. Funcraft, would the code be violated in any way?"

There was silence while the dolls considered his question.

"I don't believe so," Auntie Sarah said thoughtfully. "Myles has been throwing Mr. Funcraft pretty far away. If he couldn't find him again, he would be sad but not suspicious. He might even think he'd thrown him overboard."

"And he *will* wind up with another doll," Tiffany pointed out. "Eventually."

"We just have to figure out how to make the switch," said Mom Funcraft.

"The first part should be easy," Bobby said thoughtfully. "We'll ask Sassafras to send a message to Mr. Funcraft telling him that the next time Myles throws him out of his sight he should hide somewhere. Then when the coast is clear he should go looking for Sassafras. We'll check in with Sassafras from time to time, and when it's safe, we'll sneak Mr. Funcraft back here to the box."

"And the next part?" asked practical Nanny. "How on earth is Johnny going to take Mr. Funcraft's place without raising any suspicions? A doll doesn't simply appear from nowhere."

"That's a puzzler all right!" Tarquinius called.

Annabelle, who had been lost in thought, suddenly began to smile. "I have an idea," she said. "What if, a day or so after Mr. Funcraft has escaped, Johnny simply leaps in front of Myles?"

"*What?*" exclaimed Mama and Papa.

"*What?*" exclaimed all the other adult dolls.

"Are you mad?" cried Tarquinius.

"I am perfectly serious," said Annabelle in a dignified manner. "Myles wants an Action Man, right? So what will he think if he

sees Johnny fly onto the deck? He'll think,"
Annabelle went on without waiting for an
answer, "that he's found the perfect action
doll. After all, that's pretty much the way
he found Dad Funcraft. He won't suspect a
thing. And if he tells any of the humans what's
happened, no one will believe him. They'll
just think he has a good imagination. So all
Johnny has to do is wait somewhere—maybe
up on a deck rail, but hidden from sight, if
it's possible—until Myles walks past, and then
he can jump down onto the deck."

"Huh," said Mom Funcraft after a long
pause.

"Hmm," said Auntie Sarah after another
pause.

"That is frankly inspired!" shouted
Tarquinius.

"Annabelle, how do you think these
things up?" asked Tiffany.

"The idea just . . . came to me," Annabelle
replied modestly. She looked around at her
admiring audience, and that was when she
noticed that Otto had turned away from the
others. His shoulders were shaking. "Otto?
What's wrong?" she asked gently.

Otto hiccupped. "Nothing."

Mama Doll put her arms around him. "Tell us what's wrong."

Otto shook his head. He stepped away and sat alone on the kitten's paw.

Johnny got to his feet. He looked at Otto, then at the others, then at Otto again, and finally sat down next to his friend. "I forgot to mention one thing," he said. "It's an important part of my plan. I don't want to be Mr. Funcraft's replacement unless Otto can come with me. I'm going to need an assistant."

"You want me to be your assistant?" Otto asked incredulously. "I'll be the assistant to a superhero?"

"Absolutely," said Johnny. "Will you do it?"

"Oh, *ja!*" Otto

jumped to his feet and pulled Johnny up after him. "At your service, Johnny-on-the-Spot."

Johnny grinned. Then he removed his cape, tore it in two, and placed half around Otto's small shoulders. "Wherever I go, you go," he proclaimed. And so it was decided that Johnny and Otto would become Myles Peachy's superhero dolls.

When darkness fell that night, Annabelle looked at Tiffany. "We need to tell Sassafras our plan," she said. "And we should do it now. I think you and I should take care of that. Just the two of us."

"Why just the two of us?"

"Because . . . because we can. I thought of the plan, and, well, it's your father, Tiffany."

Tiffany considered this. At last she said, "That's true. I got us into all this trouble, and the least I can do is help bring my father back."

"Go tell the others," said Annabelle.

Tiffany hesitated. Then she stood on her tiptoes and said, "May I have your attention, please? Annabelle and I are going to go find Sassafras now and tell her the plan."

"Just you and—" Papa Doll started to say.

Tiffany interrupted him. "No arguments. We're going alone. This is something I need to do, and Annabelle is coming with me because she's brave and smart and because this was her idea."

Annabelle smiled at her friend. "Thank you," she said.

The dolls headed into the night. They found Sassafras easily, sitting abandoned in a chair not far from where they had finished their conversation with her that morning. (Had it really been only that morning? thought Annabelle. It felt like a billion years ago.) Tiffany told her their plan while Annabelle listened, not feeling the slightest bit nervous about what lay ahead. After all, Annabelle Doll had fallen down the hawse pipe and lived to tell the tale.

"Do you think we can do this?" Tiffany asked Sassafras when she had laid out the plan.

The old Tiffany, Annabelle thought, would have barged boldly ahead with the plan. The new Tiffany was cautious. Almost . . . like a fragile porcelain doll.

Sassafras nodded. "We'll have to be very

careful, of course. Johnny and Otto will most likely make their appearance during the day when lots of people are around. But I think we can carry out the plan. I can't talk to your father right away, Tiffany, because Myles took him into the cabin at bedtime, but I'll watch for him tomorrow. The moment we have a chance to talk, I'll tell him about the plan. You keep checking in with me. I have a feeling you'll have your father back very soon."

"And the rest of the plan?" said Tiffany. "Do you think Myles will be happy with Johnny and Otto?"

"More than happy. He'll have two dolls. And he'll think they're true superheroes."

"He won't be suspicious?" Annabelle wanted to know.

"I doubt it."

Annabelle and Tiffany solemnly thanked Sassafras for her help. Then they began the journey back to the ship's hold. They were sneaking down the final ramp when Tiffany said, "Annabelle, do you know, you are braver than I ever thought. You've done some brave things in the past, but today you surprised me."

"I sort of surprised myself," Annabelle replied. "When I stopped falling this morning—when the yarn on Kate's sweater ran out and I was dangling above the ocean—I barely even paused to think. I just found a way to climb back up to the hawse pipe. If you had asked me yesterday if I could have done that, I would have said no. I might even have fainted."

Tiffany laughed. "You would not have fainted!"

"No, I suppose not."

"I guess you just never know what you can do until you actually have to do it." Tiffany paused. "You also don't know what might happen to you until it actually happens."

"I think it's better not to know what lies ahead. It's good that we can't see around every corner."

"If we could, then we would always be prepared."

"And how boring would that be?" asked Annabelle. "Always being prepared for the worst? You sound like Uncle Doll."

Annabelle expected her friend to laugh, but Tiffany continued toward the pallet in silence.

CHAPTER FIFTEEN

Reunited, and It Feels So Good

E ARLY THE NEXT afternoon, Annabelle and Tiffany, hand in hand, peeked around a scuffed leather boot.

"There she is!" Annabelle said in a loud whisper. "On top of that box." Annabelle looked back and forth along the deck, which was nearly deserted. All morning long the sky had been cloudy, nearly the same color as the stormy water that was tossing *The Brown Pelican* up and down and from side to side. A chilly wind whipped Annabelle's dress about her.

"Pssst! Sassafras!" Annabelle called softly. She and Tiffany ran around the boot to the carton on which Sassafras lay.

"Have you heard from my father yet?" Tiffany asked.

It was the third visit Annabelle and Tiffany had made to the sailor doll that day. On their first visit, Sassafras, who had been sitting on a coil of rope and who had signaled frantically that Sasha was nearby, had hurriedly told them that she'd whispered their plan to Dad Funcraft just a few minutes earlier. On their second visit they'd located Sassafras, after a tiring search, on a different deck entirely, only to learn that she hadn't seen Dad again.

Now, as Annabelle stood before Sassafras for the third time, she crossed her fingers and waited for the answer she longed to hear. Please, please, please, she begged silently.

But Sassafras shook her head. "Nothing. I'm sorry. I haven't seen him."

Annabelle turned to Tiffany. "Maybe this wasn't such a good plan after all. What if—"

Tiffany interrupted her. "No what-ifs," she said.

"But there's something else," Sassafras went on. "Something important. I have to talk fast because Sasha's on her way back.

Listen to this. You're not going to believe it. Sasha got bored this morning and decided to look around the ship. She took me with her and we went down to one of the holds. And what do you think we saw? Ponies!"

"Live ponies?" asked Tiffany in amazement.

"Yes! Twelve of them, in pens. I don't know anything about them—why they're on the ship or where they're going—but when Sasha stopped to talk to one of them, I'm pretty sure I heard a little voice calling for help. A tiny little—"

"A tiny little doll voice?" Annabelle suggested.

"Yes!"

Annabelle and Tiffany stared at each other. "Bailey!" they cried.

"Where was he, Sassafras?" asked Tiffany.

"I don't know. I just heard his voice, and it was very faint. It was so faint that Sasha didn't hear it. Thank goodness."

"Where are the ponies? How do we get to them?"

"You have to—" Sassafras was saying, when suddenly she flopped onto her back. "Mayday! Mayday!" she squawked.

Annabelle snapped her head around. "Sasha's here!" she hissed to Tiffany. "Let's go!" Then to Sassafras she added, "We'll check back later."

Two tiny dolls disappeared inside a boot just as Sasha scooped up Sassafras. "Mayday! Mayday!" Sassafras continued to chirp.

Sasha rolled her eyes. "I absolutely cannot wait to get you fixed."

"Tiffany! What are we going to do?" Annabelle cried the moment Sasha had disappeared. "We have to keep checking with Sassafras to see whether she's heard from your father, and now we need to find the ponies, too."

"We could look for the ponies right now," Tiffany suggested. "We'll have to wait awhile before we check in with Sassafras again anyway."

"But we don't know where to go."

"We're searching for twelve horses!" Tiffany exclaimed. "And we know they're in one of the holds. That can't be too difficult." Tiffany had already turned and was running ahead of Annabelle, puffing hard. "Come on."

The dolls ran and ran,

down,

down,

down,

always

heading

downward.

"There's the ramp we take when we're going back to our pallet," said Annabelle.

"Let's keep going past it then," Tiffany replied. "There must be a different hold, one that we haven't been in yet."

Now the dolls crept along slowly.

"Let's try that ramp," said Annabelle, pointing. "The one at the bottom of those stairs. Keep your eyes and ears open."

The dolls crept down the ramp and listened. Nothing.

"All I see are more pallets," said Annabelle.

They returned to the top of the ramp.

"Where are we now?" Annabelle asked a few minutes later.

"I don't know. Why?"

Annabelle came to a stop and leaned against the wall, catching her breath. "Because over there," she said, "is another ramp. It looks exactly like the ones that lead to the cargo hold. And," she went on, her nose in the air, "I smell something weird. Maybe it's the ponies. Do ponies smell?"

Tiffany shrugged. Then she put her hand to her ear. "Listen for a minute."

The dolls paused and listened. "I hear neighing," said Annabelle.

"Come on, then!" Tiffany grabbed Annabelle's hand, and they scurried down the ramp.

"Wow," Annabelle whispered. "Look. There really are twelve ponies."

"They're so big," said Tiffany. "Bigger than I imagined."

"I wonder what they're doing on a ship."

"I don't know. But the air is a lot nicer here. It's cooler than the part of the hold where the ATC boxes are stowed."

"I don't see any people," said Annabelle. "Do you?"

Tiffany shook her head.

The dolls tiptoed alongside the pony pens. "Bailey!" they called softly. "Bailey! Can you hear us? Are you down here?"

Annabelle was imagining what it would feel like to be stepped on by a pony, when she heard a small voice. "Help!" it called.

She came to a halt. "Tiffany, I heard him! I heard Bailey!"

"Help!" the voice shouted again.

"Bailey?" cried Tiffany.

"Tiffany? Is that you?"

"Yes! Annabelle's here too. We're going to rescue you."

"Really? I can't believe it's you!" exclaimed Bailey. "It *is* you, isn't it? You're really here?"

"We're really here. But where are *you*?"

"In here!"

"In where? You sound like you're above us."

"I'm up in this trough. Floating around. I can't get out because the sides are too high. And they're slippery."

Tiffany tilted her head up and saw a large

227

metal water trough. "How did you get in there?"

"It's a long story."

"And we don't have time to hear it now," said Annabelle. "Sorry, but we don't. Tiffany, we have to figure out how to rescue him." She raised her voice. "Bailey, we'll be back for you as soon as we can! We're going to get help. Don't worry. We'll think of something."

Annabelle and Tiffany scrambled over each other in their rush to return to the carton. They were two boxes away from the top of the pallet when Tiffany stepped on Annabelle's hand.

"Ow!" cried Annabelle. "Tiffany, be careful. You almost made me fall."

"Girls?" called a voice from overhead. "What's going on down there? You're making an awful racket."

"Sorry, Papa," said Annabelle. "We're in a rush. We have a lot of news."

"Well, come up here slowly and tell us."

Several minutes later the dolls, including the merdolls, were assembled in the top-most carton, and Tiffany was recounting the

wondrous events of the past couple of hours.

"So we know where Bailey is," she said at last. "We just have to figure out how to rescue him. And of course we'll rescue Dad, too, as soon as he can escape from Myles."

"My goodness," said Nanny, who, Annabelle thought, still looked awfully tired. "Soon we'll all be together again. I wasn't sure that would happen."

No one bothered to mention that the reunited dolls were going to wind up more than three thousand miles from their home. Instead Auntie Sarah said, "I wonder why there are twelve ponies aboard *The Brown Pelican*."

Annabelle shook her head. "That's what Tiffany and I have been wondering. Maybe Bailey will be able to tell us."

"Only if we come up with a rescue plan quickly," said Uncle Doll. "Everybody think!"

A long silence followed.

"Think, think, think," muttered Freya.

Annabelle frowned. She thought and frowned and thought some more, until finally she noticed that Tiffany was staring at her.

"What?" said Annabelle.

"Your sweater," said Tiffany. "You aren't wearing it. Where is it?"

"You mean my wool collar? I took it off. I couldn't carry all that yarn around with me."

"But where is it?"

"Over there." Annabelle pointed to a corner of the carton. "Why?"

"Because I know how we can use it to rescue Bailey."

"Everybody ready?" asked Auntie Sarah.

"Yes!" came a chorus of doll voices.

Only twenty minutes had passed, and already Team Port, Team Starboard, and Team Merdoll were poised for action.

"Let's move out, then," said Auntie Sarah.

The members of Team Starboard left the carton first, taking Annabelle's pile of yarn with them. "Bailey, here we come!" Tiffany sang.

Team Starboard was followed by Team Port, whose assignment was to find Sassafras again and see whether she had heard from Dad Funcraft. The merdolls were to stay behind in the carton, ready to be of assistance

should either of the other two teams need them.

"We'll have to work quickly," Tiffany said, sounding excited, as her team approached the pens. "We don't know when someone might show up to check on the ponies. Does everybody know what to do?"

"Yes," said Annabelle, Mom Funcraft, and Auntie Sarah.

"All for one and one for all?" said Tiffany.

"All for one and one for all!"

"Doll power!" added Annabelle.

The ponies snorted in their pens.

"First thing—we need to find something

to fasten to one end of the yarn to give it some weight," said Tiffany. "Everybody look around."

"Here's a bolt," said Annabelle. "A bolt with a nut around it. Will this work?"

Tiffany hefted the bolt in her hands and then tied the yarn to it. She nodded. "That should do." She stepped away from the trough and yelled, "Bailey! Can you hear me?"

The ponies stamped their feet.

"Yes!" Bailey called back.

"Okay. I have a long piece of yarn here. I'm going to throw one end of it into the trough. It's weighted, so be careful. Get ready. Here it comes."

Tiffany heaved the bolt into the air. It hit the rim of the trough and fell onto the floor of the hold.

"Darn," said Tiffany. She threw the bolt a second time, and again it fell to the floor. "It's so heavy," she puffed.

"Here," said Annabelle. "Let me help you."

The two dolls gripped the bolt.

"Heave ho!" called Auntie Sarah.

The bolt sailed into the air and over the edge of the trough.

"Incoming!" shouted Tiffany, and the bolt landed with a clunk.

One of the ponies let out a neigh.

"We have to hurry," said Mom Funcraft. "If the ponies make too much noise, someone is bound to come check on them."

"Bailey!" shouted Tiffany. "Untie the yarn from the bolt and tie it to something inside the trough. Something sturdy."

"There's a metal rod in here," Bailey called back. "Just a sec."

Annabelle waited, nervously watching the ponies.

"Okay!" said Bailey.

Tiffany grasped the other end of the yarn. "Everyone hold on tight," she said to the others. "We want to keep the yarn taut. Bailey!" she shouted. "Climb up the yarn to the top of the trough. Then you can slide down it. We're waiting for you at the bottom."

Annabelle watched the trough, and presently Bailey's head appeared at the rim, followed by his arms. He pointed to something, and Annabelle realized that he had unscrewed the nut from the bolt and hauled it up with him. He had threaded the yarn through it. Bailey grasped the nut in both hands and sailed down to the floor of the hold on his very own zip line.

Annabelle stared. Then she began to smile.

I might like

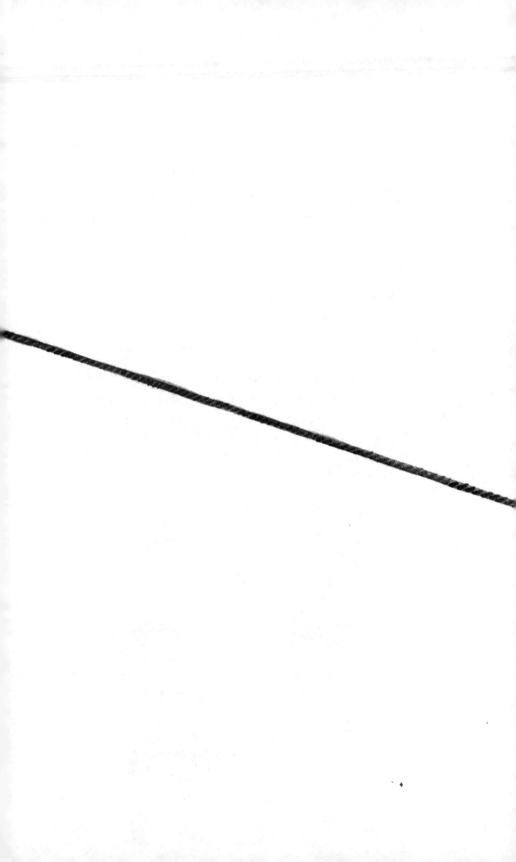

to try something like that myself sometime, she thought.

Bailey let go of the nut, and Mom Funcraft hugged him and began to cry. Then Tiffany threw her arms around him.

"Ew! Ew!" cried Bailey, but Tiffany wouldn't let go of her brother.

Annabelle watched them for a moment before yanking the yarn in two and gathering up Bailey's zip line. She looked ruefully above her head at the ragged length that now dangled from the trough. She knew she shouldn't leave it behind, but she had no choice.

Besides, Bailey was safe. That was the most important thing.

* * *

It was a laughing, happy group of dolls that made its way from the pony pens back to the ATC pallet. Everybody had questions and everybody had stories to tell.

"Where's Dad?" Bailey wanted to know as they trotted along.

"How long have you been in the water trough?" asked his mother.

"Why are the ponies on the ship?" asked Auntie Sarah.

The members of Team Starboard told Bailey what had happened since he had fallen through the hole in the box, and Bailey, puffing because he'd been cooped up in the trough and wasn't used to exercise, told his rescuers how he had wound up in the hold of *The Brown Pelican* with twelve ponies.

"You'll never guess where I landed when I flew through the hole," he began. "On a bale of hay."

"A bale of hay!" exclaimed Tiffany. "Oh, for the ponies."

"Yup. They're actually miniature ponies, and they're from a farm in Exmoor, England. They've been in a miniature horse show in

Connecticut, and now they're on their way home. Anyway, when I landed on the hay I burrowed inside so I wouldn't be seen. The next thing I knew, the bales were being moved into the hold where the ponies were staying—their pens are in a fancy climate-controlled area—and when my hay bale was tossed into the pen, I flew off and landed in the water trough. I've been avoiding pony lips for days."

Annabelle thought of pony lips and didn't know whether to laugh or scream.

The dolls had been hurrying along past the cartons in the hold, Bailey limping because of his missing shoe, and now they reached the ATC pallet. "Home sweet home," said Tiffany. "Our box is the one on top."

Bailey tipped his head back and looked up. And up and up. "You mean I have to climb all the way up *there*?" he exclaimed.

"Yes," said Annabelle solemnly. Then she added, "Follow me."

"And I'll follow Bailey," said Tiffany, "in case he slips."

The climb took a long time. Annabelle kept glancing at the hole in the top carton. The first time she looked, the hole was empty except for the flag. The second time she looked, Freya was peering down at her. The third time she looked, her mother and Bobby had joined Freya.

"Team Port is back," Annabelle announced.

"What?" said Bailey.

"We'll explain later."

Annabelle reached the carton and crawled through the hole. The moment she was inside, Bobby grabbed her and put his hand over her mouth. "Shh!" he said. "Don't say anything." He turned her around and Annabelle saw Dad Funcraft. "We want to surprise Tiffany and Bailey," he went on. "Keep quiet."

Annabelle stood back with the merdolls and watched the hole. She saw Bailey's hands grip the carton, and she heard Tiffany call to him, "Haul yourself up and crawl inside!"

When Bailey Funcraft at last was standing on the wads of tissue, he found himself facing his father. Annabelle expected shouting and screaming and jumping up and down. Instead Bailey and his father hugged each other word-lessly. They were still hugging when Tiffany's face appeared in the hole. She saw her father and almost lost her footing. Annabelle lunged for the hole and pulled her friend through.

"Dad." Tiffany's voice was no more than a whisper. She scrambled to her feet but stood back from her father. "I'm sorry," she said. "It was all my fault, and I'm sorry."

"What was all your fault?"

"The hole." Tiffany pointed over her shoulder. "I kept making it bigger, just so I could see through it better. If I hadn't done that, you wouldn't have fallen out. None of you would have." Tiffany turned from her father to look at Bailey and then at Nanny. Finally she sank onto the paw of the kitten, buried her head in her arms, and began to cry. "I'm sorry, I'm sorry," she murmured.

"Tiffany," said her father at last, "it's okay. You didn't do it on purpose." He knelt next to her. "I mean, you didn't expect any-one to fall through the hole, did you?"

Tiffany raised her head. "No, of course not."

"Then stop blaming yourself. We're all back, and we're all safe. And from what I understand, you've been very brave. You fig-ured out how to rescue your brother."

"Annabelle has been even braver," said Tiffany. "She was the true brave one."

"You're both brave," Bobby spoke up.

"You think I'm brave?" asked Annabelle in amazement.

"This is getting mushy," said Bailey.

Poseidon made a face. "Yeah, everybody's blubbering."

"We're all together again," said Mom Funcraft. "We should be happy."

"We are happy," said Annabelle.

"Now, if we can just figure out how to get back to Connecticut," said Uncle Doll, and retreated to the nest.

CHAPTER SIXTEEN

Freedom!

"**P**SSST! JOHNNY! OTTO!**" called Annabelle. "Get ready! Here comes Myles."

It was a quiet morning, the day before *The Brown Pelican* was to reach the Scilly Isles. The storm was long past and the sun was shining again. The sea was calm and the ship sailed smoothly east. Annabelle and Tiffany were huddled behind a plastic bucket on the deck outside the wheelhouse. Perched on the rail above them were Johnny-on-the-Spot and his faithful companion, Otto. And, just as Sassafras had assured the dolls would happen, Myles Peachy was now approaching the wheelhouse, scuffing his feet and frowning out at the ocean.

"Myles doesn't look very happy, does he?" murmured Tiffany.

Annabelle shook her head. "We knew he wouldn't be, not after he lost your father." She paused. "This had better work," she added, and crossed her fingers.

The dolls peered up at Johnny and Otto. Annabelle gave them the thumbs-up sign. Johnny grinned back. He gripped Otto's hand.

Tiffany kept her eyes on Myles. Suddenly she waved her arms at the superhero dolls and mouthed, "Go!"

"Oh, I can't look," Annabelle whispered, and she closed her eyes. But she opened them again just in time to see Johnny and Otto, hand in hand, leap from the ship's rail. They landed five inches in front of Myles Peachy's feet.

Myles jerked to a stop just before he stepped on Otto. "What—" He leaned over and picked up the dolls. "Where did you come from?" He examined their polka-dotted capes and Johnny's T-shirt. "J-O-T-S," he

read slowly. He looked at the capes again. "You must be superheroes," he said in awe. "Because you can really fly. I *saw* you fly. Dad! Dad!" Myles shouted. Holding one doll in each hand he disappeared inside the wheelhouse.

Annabelle and Tiffany watched from their hiding place. The last thing they saw before the door closed behind Myles was Johnny's waving hand and Otto's smiling face.

That afternoon the dolls, minus Johnny and Otto, sat anxiously in the top box of the ATC pallet.

"Tomorrow is your big day," Mama said to the merdolls. "Are you ready?"

Freya smiled. "We're ready. We're nervous, but we're ready. This is our only chance to follow our dream."

In the nest Uncle Doll looked at the babies and murmured, "I hope nothing goes wrong. There are so *many* things that could go wrong."

"Remember," said Annabelle, "that it's important to go down the anchor chain slowly. *Very* slowly. It's slippery."

"If we fall, we fall," said Poseidon, shrug-
ging. "We're headed for the ocean anyway."

"But you don't want to fall from too high
up," Bobby reminded him. "You really do
have to be careful."

"Seven seas, seven years," Freya began to
sing. "Seven merdolls, seven tears."

The other merdolls joined in. "River
to ocean: for water we yearn. Sorrow to joy,
return, return!"

"Tomorrow you shall be home," Giselle
called from the chalet.

"I hope they will be," said Annabelle.

"I know they will be," said Tiffany.

"You'd better get some rest," Mama said
to the merdolls. "You have a big day tomorrow."

"And your trial run tonight," Bobby
reminded them.

The merdolls joined hands and one by
one slipped through the hole in the carton and
returned to their box below. "We'll see you at
midnight," Freya said over her shoulder.

Now that all the missing family members had
been located, the dolls felt that they should

once again be cautious on board *The Brown Pelican*.

"No more going out in broad daylight unless we absolutely have to," Auntie Sarah had proclaimed. "We've been lucky—"

"If you consider losing three people out a hole to be lucky," Uncle Doll had muttered.

"Well, we have been lucky," Auntie Sarah had continued. "We've been out and about a lot, and we haven't been discovered. But I'd like to keep it that way."

The trial run was to be held after dark in the safety of the hold. Captain Brown planned to take the first water sample near midnight. The ship would drop anchor then and not move until the next morning, but the merdolls didn't want to make their descent into the ocean until after daybreak. Everyone agreed that leaving the ship in the dark would be much too dangerous. The merdolls needed light for their tricky trip down the chain.

"But you might as well practice first," Bobby had said, and suggested that the merdolls hold an indoor practice—scaling the full height of the ATC pallet using Annabelle's yarn—before their adventure the next day.

The length of yarn was now decidedly tatty, having already been used to rescue Bailey from the pony trough, but it would have to do.

Shortly before eleven o'clock the mer-dolls returned to the top box in the pallet, their tails tucked under their arms.

"Ready?" Annabelle asked them.

"As ready as we'll ever be," replied Freya.

"Ready, ready to return to the sea," added Seastar.

"Practice first," said Annabelle firmly.

One end of the yarn had been anchored in place by tying it to another of Kate's stuffed toys, this one wedged under several layers of toys near the bottom of the carton. "You can climb safely this way," said Mom Funcraft.

"Even if we fall, we're plastic," Neptune reminded her.

"But it would be better not to fall," replied Mom.

"Now remember," said Tiffany. "You need to bring your tails with you. And tomorrow you'll be climbing down a chain, not a piece of yarn. Keep that in mind when you practice. Okay, merdolls, take your places."

The merdolls lined up by the hole.

"I'll go first," said Dylan.

Freya glared at him. "Why? Because you're a boy?"

"No, because I want to be first." Dylan ducked through the hole before Freya could stop him.

"Okay, but tomorrow *I'm* going first!" she called after him.

Annabelle and Tiffany poked their heads through the hole and watched Dylan. He moved more slowly than they had expected.

"Oomph," he said. "This isn't easy. How am I supposed to hold on to my tail and—" At that moment his tail slipped from under his arm and fell lightly to the floor. "Uh-oh."

"What happened? Lose your tail?" bellowed Tarquinius. "You don't want that to happen tomorrow."

"No kidding," murmured Dylan.

"Let me try now," said Freya, as Dylan slid down the yarn and retrieved his tail. She paused at the opening and tied her own tail around her neck like a scarf. "There," she said triumphantly to Dylan. "That should make things easier."

Annabelle nudged Tiffany. "Dylan's blushing!" she whispered.

Freya had climbed halfway down the yarn when suddenly she paused and called up to the others. "You know what? I think climbing down the chain will actually be easier. We'll be able to step on the links for support and we won't swing around so much."

"Just remember that the chain is slippery," Annabelle cautioned her.

The rest of the merdolls made their way safely to the floor with their tails tied around their necks. Later, when they had returned to the box at the top of the pallet and the yarn had been pulled into a messy pile, which Annabelle stowed at the kitten's feet, Freya said, "All right. I guess there's nothing left to be done."

"Tomorrow," Bobby spoke up, addressing the merdolls, "you should be ready to

leave as soon as there's enough light to see by. We'll choose one of the anchor chains that's far from where Captain Brown will take the second water sample. Even so, you'll have to be very, very careful."

"We're going to go with you to see you off," added Annabelle.

"No, we're not," said Papa Doll. "Not all of us. That's much too dangerous."

"Well, I'm going," said Annabelle.

"Me too," said Tiffany.

"I think I'll stay here," said Bailey. "I hardly know you merdolls. No offense."

In the end it was decided that only

Annabelle, Tiffany, and Auntie Sarah would go along to watch the merdolls descend into their new ocean home.

The next morning the dolls gathered at dawn.

"Captain Brown gave orders to set sail again at eight o'clock," Bobby announced.

"How do you know that?" asked his mother suspiciously.

"I got word through Sassafras" was all he would say. "So let's get started."

"Right," said Freya in a businesslike manner.

"Ready?" asked Auntie Sarah.

"Yes!" chorused the excited merdolls.

"Yes," replied Annabelle and Tiffany.

Seven merdolls, their red tails tied around their necks, climbed down the ATC boxes for the last time, followed by two porcelain dolls and one plastic doll. They made their way soundlessly through *The Brown Pelican* as outside the light turned from gray to a slowly spreading pink. It was well before seven when they reached the hawse pipe that Annabelle had fallen through, and they peered inside it.

"See?" Annabelle said to the merdolls.

"The anchor chain goes through the pipe and out over the side of the ship, all the way down to the ocean."

Freya nodded.

"Climb carefully. I hope you get your wish," Annabelle went on. "I hope all your dreams come true and that you get your kingdom and your ranch and the coral reef and a seashell house and the seahorse corral."

"And maybe I'll find my sea unicorn!" exclaimed Seastar.

Auntie Sarah regarded the merdolls. She clapped her hands together smartly. "No time to waste," she said.

Annabelle hugged Freya quickly. "Good luck," she whispered. She hugged Seastar too, and then Pearl and Silver. But when she turned to the boys, Neptune ducked away from her, and the other boys said, "Ew," and wound their tails more tightly around their necks.

"Bye!" said Tiffany. "We're going to miss you."

Freya took one last look over her shoulder at Annabelle and Tiffany, and then she slipped inside the hawse pipe and grasped the anchor chain. Moments later Dylan followed her, and then one by one the merdolls crawled out of sight.

"All right. Let's go," said Auntie Sarah.

"What? *Now?*" exclaimed Tiffany. "But we have to watch the merdolls. We have to see if they get to the ocean safely."

"You are not going inside the hawse pipe," said Auntie Sarah sternly. "Not after what happened to Annabelle."

"Auntie Sarah?" said Annabelle. "I don't mean to be impertinent, but Tiffany's right. We have to make sure the merdolls are okay. We'll stay together, all three of us, and we'll hold on to the chain very tightly. We'll only go far enough so that we can see over the side of the ship."

The dolls did just that, and Annabelle was glad. They reached the end of the hawse pipe in time to see Freya, poised at the spot where the anchor chain disappeared into the water, untie her tail from around her neck, slip it over her legs, and glide into the clear green water of the Atlantic Ocean. Dylan, Seastar, Silver, Neptune, Pearl, and Poseidon were waiting for her.

"Now it really is time to go," said Auntie Sarah briskly. She turned to begin the climb back through the hawse pipe.

But Annabelle let out a gasp. "Look!" she cried.

From far, far above the water, three tiny dolls saw a glorious burst of violet as seven purple mermaid tails disappeared from view.

CHAPTER SEVENTEEN

Home at Last

THE REMAINDER OF the voyage on *The Brown Pelican* was quiet, which was fine with Uncle Doll and all the other grown-up dolls, and quick, which was fine with everyone. They were relieved that the trip was nearly over.

"There's just one thing," said Annabelle in a small voice as, at noon on a calm day, the ship sailed into the port at Plymouth, England. "What's going to happen to us now?"

No one had an answer.

Mom Funcraft shook her head. "At least we're all together again."

"And nobody was injured," added Papa.

"And those of you who lost articles of clothing got them back," said Uncle Doll.

"And we'll soon be off *The Brown Pelican*," said Nanny.

"Away from pony lips," said Bailey.

"But what will happen to us?" Annabelle asked again.

"Maybe you'll be re-homed, like Giselle and me!" shouted Tarquinius from the chalet.

"Maybe we'll all go to a new home together," Giselle suggested gently.

Annabelle didn't reply. She crept close to her mother and slid into her lap. "Our home is in Connecticut with the Palmers. Kate didn't mean to give us away."

Mama hugged her. "I know. But I suppose that whatever happens, happens. We don't have much control over things."

Tiffany had been listening to their conversation. "No," she said sadly. "We don't."

"How does that old song go?" bellowed Tarquinius. "*Que será, será*? It means 'whatever will be, will be.'"

"But this isn't what's supposed to *be*!" exclaimed Annabelle with a sob. "It just isn't."

* * *

After *The Brown Pelican* docked in Plymouth, the workers began to unload the ship.

"This is sort of like what happened at the port when we first arrived in the United States over a hundred years ago," said Bobby, trying to peer through the hole in the carton, which wasn't easy, since the adult dolls had made a rule that, from that point on, no one was to get within twelve inches of the rip.

The dolls huddled in their box as the pallet was loaded onto a forklift and trundled out of the hold and up onto a deck. Soon they felt the pallet rise into the air.

"Stand back! Stand back!" shouted Uncle Doll, not bothering to keep his voice down.

"Keep away from the hole!"

The pallet swayed and shuddered, and the dolls clung tightly to one another as they swung through the air.

"Have we landed?" asked Dad Funcraft when the swaying had stopped.

Thump.

The pallet plopped onto the ground.

Bobby stood on tiptoe exactly twelve inches from the hole and stared through it as hard as he could. He was soon joined by Annabelle, Tiffany, and Bailey.

"Look! There are your ponies, Bailey!" cried Annabelle.

The dolls watched as the ponies from Exmoor were led into what looked like very

luxurious trailers for the trip home.

The day wound on. The ATC pallet was moved several more times before Annabelle could feel the cartons being unstacked and lifted individually onto . . . what?

"Have we been loaded onto another truck?" she whispered.

"I believe," said Uncle Doll, "that here in England we are on a *lorry*."

"A lorry to where?"

"Probably to ATC headquarters," replied Auntie Sarah.

The dolls fell silent. The lorry rumbled along. Annabelle, remembering the long day of riding around in the ATC truck in Connecticut before the carton was delivered to *The Brown Pelican*, prepared herself for another interminable trip. To her surprise, after what she judged to be no more than half an hour the lorry came to a stop, the back was opened, and she heard voices and then the sound of boxes *thunk-thunk-thunk*ing as they were unloaded.

"Here we go," murmured Tiffany as their own box was lifted out of the lorry and tossed to the ground.

"Oh, now what? Now what?" whispered Annabelle. She closed her eyes and wrung her hands. For several minutes she heard nothing. Then the box was lifted yet again—this time by someone who said, "Oof. This one is heavy," before setting it gently down.

"I think we're indoors," said Bobby. He stepped closer to the hole, ignoring Uncle Doll, who was trying to grab his ankle. "I wonder how long we're going to sit here."

Not long at all, as it turned out.

Just a few moments later Annabelle was startled by a loud tearing sound, and she peered upward to see the top flaps of the carton being pulled apart.

"Burrow!" hissed Auntie Sarah, and the Dolls and Funcrafts tunneled to the bottom of the box.

"My goodness," said a woman's voice. "This one's in bad shape. One seam has split. I hope nothing fell out."

Just my nanny, my best friend's father, and my best friend's brother, thought Annabelle.

A hand reached into the box, and one by one the items with which the Dolls and the

Funcrafts had been traveling for so many days were lifted out.

"Oh, lovely!" said the voice. "Look at these plush animals. Someone will adore this kitten."

Annabelle heard the sound of another box being opened. Then a second voice, a man's, said, "This one is full of games, Deirdre. And they're all in good condition. Oh, here are some picture books."

The hand reached into Annabelle's box again. "A stuffed chipmunk. Two little puzzles. Where have you been putting puzzles, Tom?"

"Over there."

There was a soft thump, and then . . . and then . . . the hand returned to the box and closed around Annabelle herself. She didn't move a muscle as she was lifted carefully and set on a table.

"Oh! Oh, my," said Deirdre. "This is an antique doll. I'm sure of it. Come take a look at her. She's a bit disheveled." (Hmphh, thought Annabelle.) "But she ought to clean up nicely. Somebody is going to be lucky to get her."

Annabelle lay in a stiff, miserable heap on the table as one by one the other members of her family were placed around her—and the Funcrafts were set on a table across the room.

"Look what's in *this* box!" Tom called later. "Here's a little Swiss chalet with . . . well, I'm not sure what's inside. Help me pry it open."

Annabelle heard a pop as the box at last was opened.

"What funny dolls," said Deirdre. "A skinny lady in a safari outfit and a man who looks like a professor. Tiny spectacles and all."

Annabelle did something then that she knew she was absolutely not supposed to do. She slid her eyes just the teensiest bit sideways and found herself gazing at Giselle and Tarquinius. She couldn't smile, she couldn't wave, she couldn't even wink, but she looked fondly at her traveling companions and sent them a silent wish for re-homing with a child who would love them.

That was when she heard a phone ring.

"I'll get it," said Deirdre.

Annabelle longed to reach for her mother's hand. She longed to sit up and look around the room for Tiffany. But she could do nothing except lie on the table. And listen. She listened to Deirdre's end of a lengthy phone conversation.

"Yes," said Deirdre, "they've just arrived. We're unpacking them now. . . . Yes, the ones that originated in Connecticut in the United States. . . . What? . . . Oh. . . . *Oh*. . . . Well, we haven't finished unpacking everything, but I think I know what you're talking about. . . . From a box without an ATC label? Let me check." A moment later Deirdre's face hovered above Annabelle's. She set the phone down on the table and examined the box that the Dolls and the Funcrafts had been traveling in. Then she picked up the phone again. "You're right," she said. "The dolls you described came from a box that was with the other ATC boxes, but it doesn't have a label on it."

Annabelle's heart began to pound.

"Yes," said Deirdre again. "Of course . . . What? Fourteen in all? Wait a bit. Let me get a pencil and write that down. . . .

All right. Go ahead. . . . Nine antique dolls and five of the odd plastic ones? All right, I'll see if they're all here."

Now Deirdre's hand hovered above the dolls as she counted them. A moment later she said into the phone, "Got them. They're all here, as far as I can tell. Some of them look a bit tatty. I don't know if that's how they started off. The box is squashed and ripped. None of the dolls is actually broken, though." A long pause followed, and at last Deirdre said, "I'll set them aside and we'll get them packed up as soon as we can. . . . What? Oh, of course. I see. We'll repack the contents of the entire box, then."

When at last she ended the phone call, she said to Tom, "A slight mistake in the States. The carton I was unpacking wasn't supposed to come here at all. And the people who sent it want it back badly. They especially want the dolls. Let me see if I can remember everything I took out of the box."

Deirdre gathered up the Dolls, the Funcrafts, the kitten, the chipmunk, the puzzles, and the other toys, and called, "Tom? Do we have a carton that's in good condition?

I can't fly them back in the one they were packed in. It's falling apart."

Fly us back? thought Annabelle. We're going to fly on a plane? The thought was alarming. But not nearly as alarming, of course, as most of the things that had happened to Annabelle since her unexpected journey had begun.

The day after the Dolls and the Funcrafts arrived in Plymouth, they were returned to the United States.

"Just think," Tiffany said to Annabelle from within their new carton as they soared thousands of feet above the Atlantic Ocean. "Since we left the Palmers', we've traveled on a truck, a crane, a forklift, a ship, a lorry—"

"A lorry's the same as a truck," Bobby interrupted her.

"Whatever. And now we're on a plane."

"Not many dolls can say that," Annabelle replied. She remembered how upset she'd been at the thought of twiddling her thumbs in the attic while the Palmers were away. The ocean trip had been nerve-racking, but it certainly hadn't been boring.

Tiffany looked thoughtful. Finally she sighed and said to Annabelle, "At least the trip wasn't my fault."

"What do you mean?"

"I mean that I wasn't the one who mixed up the cartons. But half of what happened on the ship was because of something I did. Something I did without thinking. I just poked at the hole, and the next thing I knew, doll people were flying out of it."

"But that's understandable," said Annabelle. "You're unbreakable. You've never had to worry about what you do, because it's hard for you to get hurt."

In her mind Annabelle could hear Uncle Doll saying, "Our actions have consequences," but she refrained from repeating this to Tiffany. It wasn't the time. Annabelle was on her way home, with her family and her best friend. Soon she would be at the Palmers' house again, and soon after that—whenever the renovation was completely and thoroughly finished—she would be back in her own house in Kate's room, sleeping in her own bed.

"Well, I'm going to be much, much more careful from now on," said Tiffany.

"But not too careful," replied Annabelle. "I still want you to be Tiffany."

Many hours after the dolls left ATC headquarters in Plymouth, their new carton was delivered to the Palmers' house on Wetherby Lane. Annabelle heard the doorbell ring and then Nora's voice shouting, "I'll get it! I'll get it!"

There was some shuffling around and the sound of several voices speaking earnestly, followed by a door closing. Then quick as a flash the carton was ripped open.

Annabelle, who was lying on her back in a stew of Styrofoam bits, looked upward and saw a pair of hands digging through the box. Moments later she saw five anxious faces—Kate's, Nora's, their parents', and Grandma Katherine's—hovering above.

"They're here! The Dolls are all here!" exclaimed Kate as soon as the nine members of Annabelle's family were lined up on the floor of the hallway. She regarded them seriously. "I missed you," she said. "I missed you so much while we were at the ranch. And I was worried about you!"

"All the Funcrafts are here too," said Nora.

"Thank goodness we realized our mistake as soon as we got home," said Mrs. Palmer. "That's what we get for rushing around and doing things at the last minute."

"All's well that ends well," said Grandma Katherine kindly.

"Just think," said Kate. "The dolls went all the way to England, which is where they came from in the first place. They certainly have had a lot of adventures. Hey, Annabelle, where's your sweater?" Kate began digging through the box again, and Annabelle remembered fondly the moment at which she had finally discarded the horrible sweater-collar before Bailey's rescue.

"*I* haven't been to England," said Nora.

Kate gave up her search for the sweater. She put her hands on her hips. "Well, neither have I."

"Unfortunately, the dolls still have to go up to the attic for a little while," Mr. Palmer said to Kate and Nora then.

"But why?" asked Kate, with a slight whine to her voice. "Couldn't the dolls stay with Nora and me in the guest room until our bedrooms are ready? They probably had an awful experience while they were away. Couldn't they stay with us? Please?"

"I don't see why not," replied her mother.

Kate returned the Dolls to the carton, carried the carton upstairs, and set it in the guest room. "Sorry you can't sleep in your house. It's up in the attic. But you can sleep in here with Nora and me until everything is back to normal."

Nora followed Kate into the room and set the Funcrafts on the floor. "Look, dollies," she said. "Look what I got while we were on our trip. The Funcraft Circus Pack. You can be circus dolls! See? Here's your trapeze and here's your tightrope. Oh, and here's a palomino horse. You can be bareback riders. Okay, who wants to go first?"

Annabelle stared at the circus that Nora was setting up on the floor. Plastic animals. Flying contraptions. She heard Uncle Doll, who was lying next to her, let out a teensy moan. Moments later Nora galloped Mom Funcraft by on the palomino. She's riding bareback, thought Annabelle, but then she remembered Nanny caught on the cable high above the deck of *The Brown Pelican*, and she knew things could be a lot worse. Besides, Mom Funcraft was trying very hard not to laugh.

"Kate?" said Nora. "Could I sit Annabelle on the trapeze?"

Kate shook her head. "Better not. She's too fragile."

"Okay," said Nora. She turned away from her sister, picked up Annabelle, and whispered to her, "But someday I'm going to put you in the circus."

Annabelle found that she didn't mind
the idea one bit.

ANN M. MARTIN is the author of many books for young readers, including *Rain Reign, Belle Teal, A Dog's Life,* and *A Corner of the Universe,* a 2003 Newbery Honor Book. She is also the author of the Baby-sitters Club series and the Family Tree series. Ms. Martin makes her home in upstate New York.

LAURA GODWIN, also known as Nola Buck, is the author of many popular picture books for children, including *Oh, Cats!; One Moon, Two Cats; This Is the Firefighter;* and *Christmas in the Manger.* Born and raised in Alberta, Canada, she now lives in New York City.

BRETT HELQUIST is the illustrator of the best-selling A Series of Unfortunate Events books as well as many other popular titles. He worked as a graphic designer before becoming a full-time illustrator. Brett lives with his family in Brooklyn, New York. See more of his work online at bretthelquist.com.